CONTENTS

A PEASANT FARMER'S PSALM

FELIX TIMMERMANS (1886-1947) initially worked as a pattern drawer in his father's lace business. After World War I, he moved to the Netherlands, where he stayed until 1920, earning his living as a writer, poet, painter and artist. Although he also published poetry, plays and adaptations of medieval texts, Timmermans primarily wrote novels, fictionalised biographies and stories. In 1935, he published his well-known work, *A Peasant Farmer's Psalm*, a novel that reveals a deep knowledge of suffering, in which praise of nature gives way to praise of humanity.

PAUL VINCENT studied at Cambridge and Amsterdam, and after teaching Dutch at the University of London for over twenty years became a full-time translator in 1989. Since then he has published a wide variety of translated poetry, non-fiction and fiction, including work by Achterberg, Claus, Couperus, Elsschot, Jellema, Mulisch, De Moor and Van den Brink. He is a member of the Society of Dutch Literature in Leiden, and has won the Reid Prize for poetry translation, the Vondel Prize for Dutch-English translation and (jointly) the Oxford-Weidenfeld Prize.

SNUGGLY BOOKS

A PEASANT FARMER'S PSALM

I

I'M just a peasant farmer and though I've had my share of misery, the farmer's life is the most wonderful life on earth. I wouldn't swap places with a king.

God, I thank You for making me a farmer!

I was born over there in that cottage. There were fifteen of us open mouths, and although we sometimes got more thumps than food, it was still a childhood and we grew into men strong as tree trunks.

A large household is a joy.

I like a big bunch of kids. A good tree must bear lots of fruit.

I've never refused my wife a child. Growing things is our vocation. Children as well as cabbages. Then you know what you're living for and who you're working for. It didn't kill our father and mother. At the age of eighty she was still straight as a ramrod and, whistling all the while, would hoist a sack of potatoes into the loft. Our father had toiled until he was as crooked as a question mark. When they tried to put him in his coffin he either sat up straight or his legs stuck in the air. They had to crack him in two, or at least I did. The others were scared. The old Honourable Lady from the chateau, from whom we rented our land, often came and asked him to work for her as a gardener. Light work, good pay, and a share in the profit from the fruit.

'Nonsense!' he would say. 'A farmer must stay a farmer, otherwise the world won't go round.'

That's why he fussed and sulked, because only one out of all of us was keen to follow the farmer's trade.

I have brothers and sisters in Antwerp and Brussels, there are two in America, one in France, one in the loony bin—that can happen in the best families—and one is a monk with the barefoot friars in Dendermonde. We only see him when they need money in his monastery. That's why our dad always called me 'Our Root'. I stayed. I couldn't leave the field. It's such a magnet. The field attracts you. You love it and you don't know why.

Because looked at closely, the priest is right when he says that the field is a kind of enemy, a giant, he says, that fights against us day in, day out.

One has to oppose it body and soul. Have you ever considered what has to be done to put bread on your table?

Ploughing, fertilising, harrowing, sowing, threshing, grinding and baking. And if Our Dear Lord doesn't intervene, and if you don't bribe the saints with a candle, against the slugs, the worms, thunder and lightning, then all your sweat will have gone down the drain. But when you hold the sandwich made from the new harvest which you tore out of the ground with your own strength, in your massive hands, and you can sink your teeth in it and at the same time you see a whole table of eaters around you, it's as if the Boss upstairs puts his hand on your shoulder and whispers softly in your ear: very well done, Root, thank you!

No, to my way of thinking the field isn't a giant, but a giantess, a huge female creature that you can't see to the end of. Her face is the sky. She lures you on. You walk over her body, you crawl over it. Of course, she frustrates you like all women. That's the good thing about it. You coax and cajole her. You don't give up, and then she becomes mild and obliging, and gives and gives, and there's no stopping her!

A farmer must also have a good wife in his bed, but she mustn't stay lying in it. She must make butter, feed men and beasts, help out, work her hands to the bone till there's nothing left but elbows. I've known lots of girls, I was quite a lad in my time, I fought for them, more from love of fighting than because of the girls. I waited for the right one and the right ones are rare, and also come along unexpectedly.

Our Fine came from across the River Nete.

Strange how love conquers one's heart.

On the pilgrimage to Scherpenheuvel—I walk to Scherpenheuvel every year—there we sat in the same pub, with lots of other people, eating our sandwiches. Outside it was raining, and the floor was muddy. She was sitting opposite me but I hadn't yet noticed her. There were so many people and my mind was elsewhere, I tried to shift along a bit to let a farmer's wife through and unexpectedly knocked over my glass of beer. She jumped up to protect her dress, and her sandwiches fell on the floor. I was embarrassed and gave her three of mine. She didn't want to take them. 'Then I'll throw mine in the mud too,' I said. They had bacon in them.

Then she took them.

'Do you like them?' I asked.

'Yes,' she said, 'it's really good bread.'

'Where do you live?'

We got talking. She shone like a dry onion. She was a full-figured, buxom woman. I would have liked to go back with her, but she was with her family.

I couldn't get her out of my thoughts, I saw her in front of me the whole time: in the field when I ate, and I dreamt such lustful dreams about her.

I couldn't find rest or peace of mind, and whenever I could I went to the Nete in the evenings. From there you could see the tiled roof of her house. I lay smoking one pipe after another and kept whistling the tune of 'Ave Maria' to make her think of Scherpenheuvel and me, and come and see what was up. No such luck.

But the next Sunday I see her coming from mass along the other bank with her sister.

'Well,' I shouted brazenly, 'did you like the sandwiches?'

She began giggling and laughing. I got very embarrassed, but still shouted, 'Can I bring you a whole loaf shortly? We baked only yesterday!'

12

They ran down the bank, along the verge. She looked round once.

'I'll be back tomorrow,' I said, encouraged by this.

I waved my hand. She waved back. I felt it was going well, and my heart was so restless that I couldn't sit in the same pub for five minutes.

The next day then, towards evening I took all my courage in both hands and my bread wrapped in a towel, and without saying a word I was gone. It's an hour's detour through the town. I open the door. There sit her brothers, five of them, and her father, a man built like a pillar. They were eating potatoes from the pan. I didn't say much. Just that I had brought a loaf for that one over there. I didn't know her name yet. She sat there looking ashamed and was close to tears. I don't know how, but before I could count to three I was outside lying thrashing about with my legs in a canal. They'd kept my loaf. I heard them laughing. One against six was no good, I was like a sack of broken pipe stems. I just crawled home, but as you can understand raging like a tiger, and with the firm resolve to have my revenge *and* the girl.

At home I spoke to my three brothers about it, quietly.

The next day the four of us stood sharpening our knives on the whetstone. By the time it was pitch dark, we were over there. Her brothers, who were home at the time, called for pen and ink, without us having to use our knives. She was so alarmed she dropped the washing-up. And while my brothers beat her brothers, I said to her, I said to her: 'The ground will be red with blood unless you become my love!'

13

Her sister had run out and called for help, but before that help arrived, with dogs and pitchforks, we jumped into the Nete, and stood jeering at them jauntily from the other side.

I was going mad. I felt I had made a mess of everything. I was not fit for work anymore. I spent every day spying on her house from behind the irises. If she loves me, she'll come and take a look sometime, because our cottage is easy to find from there.

One Saturday, when I was about to give up on her, I was lying there again, and I saw her coming down the path to draw water. When she had filled the first bucket, I called out: 'Hey there!' She went pale. She didn't dare shout, but motioned with her hand for me to go away.

'I'm coming!' I cried, 'wait!'

I took off my cap and swam across. She was rooted to the spot with fright. She started to cry because she was so pleased to see me. We sat down together for a bit. And you know how it goes, you're both young and on fire, and they work against you, which makes things worse, and you don't talk about sandwiches any more. I'm in seventh heaven and have already swum back. That evening I sang so much the neighbours thought I was mad. We met several more times in the evenings. It was haymaking time. The haycocks are lush and smell so good. And what I had suspected came to pass. A month or so later her father came to see us. He had to speak to me. I kept my cleaver at the ready, and he asked me what I intended: marrying or not, and the sooner the better!

'Yes,' I said, 'but with a horse and a cow thrown in.'

He took the bait. It was a lovely wedding. And our late Dad danced with delight.

'You pulled a fast one on him there, Root,' he said.

That first night! They had hung bells beneath our bed, and our Fien had probably had a drop too much to drink and complained of a severe headache. I wasn't fooled. I thought, I've got time enough. I went for a walk in the moonlight. The corn was ready to be harvested, and is there anything nicer than corn to sleep in? I lay down somewhere and looked up at the stars. I often like looking at them. You see something completely different. Your heart grows still and you think of things you don't have time for otherwise. Of Our Dear Lord, who created all that and of the insignificance of your own life. The priest says the stars are as big as planets. Paper is patient, but as soon as I lay there, I felt something great and solemn come over me. Like in church sometimes and then I promised myself always to do my duty as well as I could to God and everyone.

The next day when the sun came up I stood picking corn with our Fien where I had slept the very same night.

Then the misery began. At about seven o'clock Fien went to fetch coffee and sandwiches, and we had only just sat down, when at the first bite she started screaming: 'I can't go on, my head weighs like lead.' She had to go home. I was left alone. Struggling against the burning sun and a big swathe of corn.

That was a wretched experience, that pain in the head! And if you don't feel it at all, you think it's play-acting, make-believe. Then harsh words are sometimes exchanged. That headache has cost us lots of money and shoe leather. The doctor, the piss doctor, Aloiske the magician and what a succession of pilgrimages! I scarcely ever saw her without a white cloth and something round her head.

Others laughed at it.

Once we went to Peuthy. She came back cured and in two weeks had not a second of pain.

Then she said: 'Root, I'm cured. We must give something to our priest in thanks.'

We had just killed our pig and I proudly took the head to our priest.

'Very good,' he said, 'but why a head?'

'Because my head's cured.'

He said, 'a shame you didn't have pain somewhere else, then I'd have got a nice pair of hams.'

He's a good man, though, our priest, an upright soul, a saint, sometimes. Because he has a maid who bosses him about and sometimes makes him explode with fury. He likes being given things, he's keen on that, but on the other hand he gives away the shirt off his back. Life is no laughing matter, he always says, though I've never yet seen him cry. He often drops in to see me. Then he always gets a pint of milk, straight from the udder. If we're in the field, I call out: 'Help yourself!' Then he goes into the cowshed himself to draw off a pint… or two. If one's not there! The priest knows me inside out. He follows and consoles us in our misery and our poverty. And every year at Easter I shake out my basketful of sins over his head. I always promise to mend my ways, but a man isn't made of stone. Our Dear Lord has scattered us across the world with our shortcomings. He must simply take us back as we are. Of course, we mustn't go too far. Eliminating all our shortcomings is a job for moaners and hypocrites. A farmer who does his duty has other things to eliminate: thistles and weeds among the potatoes and the caterpillars that eat your apples. The field gives us no time or opportunity to stand against a pillar with a gold plate behind our head. And yet there was a St. Isodore, whom I often called on. While he sat praying, the angels sowed and ploughed for him. I've never tried it, because I'm happy I can get the work done with my own hands.

It was a hard year, that first one, and the second was harder still. High in rent. The frail lady from the chateau said, 'Young people are worth a little more, since they can work harder.'

Our cow was due to calve, and with a great effort we managed to drag the calf out of the cow alive, but the cow succumbed.

I burnt my foot, the bare flesh, as I was boiling pig feed. Sat on a chair for two weeks. It drove me up the wall. That wretched pig! When we killed it, the priest brought the six cutlets back. 'Life is no laughing matter,' he said, 'but your pig is a male with undescended testicles.' A faint, bitter gall-like taste. We were stuck with it for the whole winter. To give more variety to the flavour I went poaching at night.

The winter was harsh, the ground was like freestone, it broke the strongest fork, no way to get the turnips and the beets out of their holes. A comet came out of the sky. The farmers were all a-tremble. We kept an eye on the fields, and on the dark clouds that came from over the Nete and brought constant new snow. Then it was hurricanes that shook our little house so that I didn't dare go to bed without my trousers on. Our roof ruined and those apple-trees snapped in two. It thundered in midwinter. But nothing can last for ever. On Shrove Tuesday it started to thaw and it poured with rain for days on end. The fields were a mess of porridge. The southern side remained dark and sodden. An evil quarter, that south. And then came the blow. It was the comet that did that to us.

The Nete broke its banks. All the fields were under water, and our winter corn came floating in over my threshold. And that same evening, as we stood up to our ankles in the water, our little Polleken was born. Produced on the water and born above the water. And best of all, I had had to bring the animals from the cowshed, except for the horse, which was big enough, but the calf, the goat, the young pig and the rabbits, into the house, otherwise they would have drowned. The animals witnessed what went on too. Bell Salamander, the maid-of-all-work among our neighbours, came to help. Everyone had enough work fishing for pots and pans in their own yards. The water crept silently upwards. Our little Polleken didn't have an easy birth.

I had my heart in my mouth and I forgot the flood when I saw how our Fine was suffering. Bel Salamander said: 'God doesn't give people more pain than they can bear.' Or till they die of it, I thought to myself. Then I felt so truly how much I loved my wife. I regretted all my angry words, and by God, as big a man as I am, I kneel down in the water and call to Our Dear Lord, like a little child. But then Bel cried out:

'Little chicken cock, give the child a frock!' She stuck our little Polleken under my nose. Our Fien laughed and I laughed. I've seldom felt so happy. Then the priest came in with his cassock rolled up, wellingtons on and a pipe in his mouth.

'Congratulations, Root,' he said, 'you'll have to call the baby Moses, because the water is subsiding.'

There followed two miscarriages. Our consolation was that God let us keep little Polleken. But not for long. I still can't swallow the fact that Our Dear Lord did that to me. And if I am admitted to Heaven I want to ask Him in my own words what I did to deserve that. Perhaps He had His reasons. I must know what they were. Otherwise, I can't simply join in the Hallelujah chorus.

Ha! He was a beautiful child; I'm not surprised with milk like my wife's. I could listen and look until my pipe went out when the baby lay on her lovely big breasts. And then there were his little red hands that scrabbled across them like red beetroot, then you go all soft, and you need to swear a bit to become a man again.

I've never sung much, but to get him to sleep I could easily spend a whole hour whining at his cradle, and our dog was so het up he joined in the whining. On Sunday morning, when people can have a bit more of a lie-in, I let the baby crawl over my body and tug at my hair and moustache so that it brought tears to my eyes.

He was so smart and quick-witted! He played with the cat and the dog. He rocked with laughter when he was able to pull our pig's tail. He sat with me on our horse, close to me with my pipe in his mouth. I took him with me as much as possible to the field, to the pub, on Sunday walks. I was mad about the child. And the things I knocked together for him. Wooden puppets, ducks that could float, and a little windmill.

We were approaching winter. In March our little Polleken would be two. I was just in the cart shed bundling carrots. Our little Polleken was standing by. Suddenly there's a skinny old woman in front of me, selling matches.

'Do you need any matches?'

I still had some matches. Our Fien gave her a slice of bread filled with sweet dripping.

'What a beautiful child,' said the woman, like a bleating goat, and she stroked our little Polleken's head.

She goes away and less than a quarter of an hour after she's left the yard, the child starts to go red. He groaned so pitifully and looked as cross-eyed as an otter. Straight to the doctor. The stupid fool said: 'Ate too much,' and prescribed a bottle of something. That bottle made things worse. A coal fire was no hotter than he was. I fetched the priest. He read something from his book and made signs of the cross. Bel Salamander laid a medal of St Benedict on his heart and lit a candle from Lourdes. I had Aloiske, the exorcist, sent for. 'The evil hand,' he said, 'go to Kruiskensberg, and provided all the wells are not empty he'll recover, if every week for a whole year you read Emperor Charles' prayer on Friday.'

I went to Kruiskensberg. What luck! The wells were full, I no longer know how I got home. It was as if I flew over bushes and hedges. But when I opened the door, our Pol was lying dead in our Fien's lap. He looked green.

The weeping and lamenting that went on in that little cottage!

There was a thick fog when Bel Salamander took the deal coffin, which I had made myself, to the cemetery. I went with her. When I saw the coffin being laid in the earth, I cursed and shouted. The grave-digger pulled such a sad face that I gave the chap twenty cents. But he said: 'Be happy, Root, he's an angel in heaven.' I gave the fellow a blow that made him spin round. I had to forget the pain in my heart. We drowned our sorrows in 'The Last Farewell', so that Bel had to take me home at noon in a wheelbarrow.

But then! The house is empty. There was a child here. Your voice climbs up to the roof tiles. You no longer dare speak aloud. You say nothing about the child in order not to inflict pain on each other, and what else can you speak about? That silence, that silence. Death creaks on the stairs. The child has gone, that beautiful child. He lies locked in earth over there and still you expect it at any moment and you prick your ears up to hear his laughter and his shouting. It's seven o'clock, that was his bedtime, you think, it's four o'clock now let's have an early sandwich with syrup.

The dog looks for him, He snuffles at the shoes, looks at us, looks at the shoes again and goes outside to search for our Polleken.

'Where's our little Polleken?' you hear your wife ask the dog. Then you have to curse or leave. And those toys! You hide them in the loft, although you are more inclined to put them in your glass case. My wife once sat kneeling by them. Then I put a sheet over them. But when I was at home alone, I crept up to the loft and made the horse swing and the windmill turn. I started drinking. But at a certain moment I thought back to the stars and the promise of the night I got married. I poured the bottles of gin onto the dung heap. It was a broken household, I could no longer handle the work. Yet work is necessary.

We were planting beet in the field. And again I saw her tears flowing.

And see, she fell to her knees. 'Now I haven't got a baby anymore, now we haven't a baby anymore!'

My feelings were full to overflowing. I pulled her up, took her in my arms and promised her another baby. That gave her fresh courage.

I've always done my duty. That's why you're a man and a human being. Thank God!

II

GOD asks for children. He gets them.

They were a healthy pair of twins. From then on Fien's womb was never empty, so to speak. Sowing, mowing. Our Fien could handle it in spite of her headache. Where there are two, there's room for three, Root.

'And so on,' I said.

We were soon up to our ears in children. If only our Polleken was still part of the bunch!

People seem to love dead children more than the living. The living ones have to pull their weight and from time get a smack on the bum that makes your hand tingle. You moan and whine at them. They are your burden, your worry. They keep you poor and shut you up in a tower of trouble. But if there's any-thing wrong with them, or you have bad dreams about them, or you are in jail for poaching, you realise how dear those toddlers are to your heart. You wouldn't want to lose a single one for a million francs, you'd go through fire for them, and sometimes they make you so mad you could bash their heads in.

You think: God, You've asked for children for Your greater Glory, here they are, as many as You want, but I beg you, make sure they don't cost me my own glory!

Life is no laughing matter, and yet who would want to die, O Lord! For you gave me children, one of them is even blind from birth, and you gave me the field. Two gifts that are hard to bear. A farmer is tied to his field, it's as if he's chained to it. A farmer lives to work. Every day the field wakes him up.

It may be a piece of rough ground, as God breathed it out, brutal and unmanageable, like everything you've received from Him.

A piece of brutal, rough land. You can turn your back and leave it where it is, and go to work in the harbour. Then you'll sleep like an ox at night. But if you just stick your finger in the ground, you are dragged along body and soul as if by wheels and pulleys. Then that plot of land is your life.

Day and night. Out of bed while it's still dark, in the rain and hail or the scorching sun, constantly bending forward or crawling while digging, weeding, cutting back, planting, harvesting, threshing in the last glimmer of light. Planting leeks is a torture in itself. Another man sleeps like a log and dreams of lambs and cake, but the farmer, however exhausted, still sleeps with one eye open. He listens to hear whether rain is on the way, or whether it is soon going to stop. He can see all his offspring in front of him, feels them as something belonging to him, like his own fingers. They yearn for this, or complain about that. The farmer's heart complains or yearns along with them. He gets up, pokes his head outside; he studies the moon and the clouds, feels for the wind and listens to his animals, he occasionally makes water on the dung heap, nothing must be wasted, dung is a demi-god, and then he crawls back in behind his farmer's wife, and waits for morning. That's how it goes, day in, day out, year after year, a whole lifetime: buckets of sweat, blisters on your hands, scabs on your knees and later a hunchback.

It won't make you rich. The owner of the chateau won't allow that. He has to have his parties.

You know all that, and yet because of the enchantment of your farmer's blood you spit in your hands. God bless us! And you plant the spade in the ground.

From then on you're the slave of the field, just as you're the slave of your children.

In the centre is the wife. Our Fien, the mother.

She keeps us together. Everything revolves around her. She keeps the household in order, the children, our heart. Me too, except for Sundays. Then I come singing and waddling home, then I'm my own man. I feel rich, a master, great, happy and good like St. Francis. Our Fien doesn't complain, she approves: our Root must be able to give his senses their due sometimes.

The children come rolling out of her womb like turnips. They suck at their glasses, grow thanks to her good milk. They play on her lap, lie in her arms, sleep next to her heart. They come and cry on her lap. They die in her lap. She attracts the children and the husband. She keeps me young like an English cockerel. You have your suit on and all your gear, but that's not the most remarkable thing, because then you could have the first woman who came along. There's still something between you and her, something from heart to heart, that no pen can describe. It's that that ties you to her and gives you both the strength to bear much grief and misery. Yes, why this woman and no other? God wrote it in the stars. You are proud of your wife, wish everyone would come and say: Root, you made a good choice! But people are put together in a strange way, because if anyone looks on her with lecherous eyes, which is understandable, you'd like to tear the fellow apart.

For instance, I once had a spot of bother with the Oxhead. The Oxhead lives in my neighbourhood, two farms further on in the direction of the village. Our fields are adjacent. He came over to our place a lot, and I went over to his. I have quite a temper. Provided no one gets in my way, I'm as good as gold, a sucker even, but if they hurt me, spitefully, then I lose sight of God and the devil. Well, the Oxhead preferred dropping into our place when I wasn't there. I didn't like that. The Oxhead was known as someone for whom all cats are grey in the dark. But I let that pass. Fien's a serious person, and surely he wouldn't want to do the dirt on his best mate? But on one occasion, when we were both in bed awake, our Fien says: 'Root, we have to put a stop to that Oxhead, he won't leave me alone.'

I jumped up like lightning, without taking the time to put my trousers on, and went over to the table drawer and grabbed a breadknife, but our Fien was already standing with her back against the door.

'Root, Root, think of your children, for god's sake don't be a murderer!'

I could scarcely see her in the dark, but her pitiful voice cut me to the quick:

'Don't be a murderer, think of your children!' I pulled her out of the way, she held me tight by my legs, and she pleaded, she pleaded: don't be a murderer!

'All right,' I shouted, 'but let me break or smash something then or I shall choke!'

She immediately lit the lamp and gave me six plates from the cupboard.

'Here you are, Root, just smash them to bits, lad.' Bang, wham, crash, the pieces flew round like hailstones.

Then she gave me a china coffee pot, a wedding present. Straightaway smashed to smithereens on the floor! 'Look here, Root, as long as you don't commit any murders, she said with tears running down her face, and she gave me a tray with six glasses on it. Wham, they were also smashed to smithereens! The children in the attic started awake and began screaming.

'Haven't you finished yet, Root?' she sobbed. And she hands me the jar of fat and the bottle of vinegar.

She would have let the whole house be smashed to pieces to avoid a murder. Ah! What a good, lovely wife! I suddenly realised. It was as if my arms were paralysed.

'Come on,' I said. Back in our bed I took her in my arms, so happy was I that she'd saved me from the devil. Then we fell asleep. But at about two o'clock, when I woke as usual, and went outside in my night-shirt, my rage flared up. I didn't want to be a murderer and tomorrow I was bound to be one! How would it end if that fellow appeared again in my sight? My fingers were open, ready to claw him. By God, by God, I can't stop myself! In the dark I saw the axe gleaming in the cart shed. It seemed to leap into my hands and I started cutting and cleaving everything that came to hand, in order to calm down. Suddenly I hear: 'Is that you, Root? It was Franelle from next door, who had woken up because of me.

'Yes, Franelle.'

'Have you gone mad, Root?'

'Almost.'

He came down and meanwhile I hear the Oxhead.

'Franelle, is that you, or Root?'

'It's Root,' called Franelle.

They both stood in front of me. I cut and cleaved for all I was worth.

'What's got into you?' asked the Oxhead.

'If you value your skin, Oxhead, stay five steps away from me and my wife, or else…'

'I don't understand you, Root.'

'I understand you, and now you've been warned, Oxhead.'

Are you saying I'm a thief?'

That's how we talked to each other. I boiled over.

Now it was going to happen. My guardian angel, hold me in check!

The sweat was leaking onto my face from suppressed rage, I had to murder. Oxhead poured oil on the flames.

'Do you hear me, Franelle? Root is making me out to be a thief. You'd better take those words back, Root.'

'I haven't put anything forward, and I'm not taking anything back, but if you don't keep your hands to yourself, I'll cut them off. Look, that's how I'll do it, Oxhead!'

I picked up a block. I cut it in two in a trice.

'Those are your hands!'

I pick up another block which I cut down the middle.

'Those are your legs.' I take piece of trunk. 'And that's your head, Oxhead.' A swing, but the axe got stuck. I looked up. Franelle and the Oxhead had vanished.

Not a murderer! That had gone off beautifully. I could have knelt before God like in church, but I was too shy, with no trousers on.

The Oxhead never again crossed my threshold. He wasn't such a fool as to ask for an explanation. For the rest we still talked to each other, at a distance, and there was a sulky air between us.

So a man must always be suspicious and on watch, to keep his field, his wife and his children and himself safe.

On all sides life lurks, waiting to trip you up. The heart cannot rest and there is always a rush in your blood.

People are fond of lecturing others, as if they have a shop selling virtues, yet they have to watch their own step to avoid being washed down the plughole themselves.

I wanted to cleave the Oxhead and for a long time after I could have done it to myself.

Whenever I took my corn to the mill, I always stopped off at the Twister's place, to smoke a pipe and have a chat. The Twister, a widower, has four cows and a quality bull, but only two children. The former maid had got married and now he had a new one. A youthful puss, a delight to behold. Enough to make you forget purgatory and hell. 'Congratulations, Twister,' said everyone and winked. But the Twister was dried up, made of straw. He had no eyes for that. Now the maid was there I was even more inclined to stop off. Her laughter went on echoing in your ribs like in a church and her black eyes lured you on like corn. A man is not an idle watchman and I began to put my mind to it, looked for excuses to go to the Twister's place. I occasionally pinched her arms, and she just laughed seductively. I could no longer control myself and began to think of ways: How am I to get hold of her? But then our priest, on Sunday, preached on the sixth commandment so passionately and beautifully, that I resolved to stay away from the Twister. I was just glad that I had realised my mistake in time. When in the afternoon I walked alone through the field, I could have cried out with regret at my sinful intentions and yet I peered around hornily to see if I could spot her, and at the same time I was glad not to see her!

God, how curiously You constructed man.

He's held together with hooks and eyes. And the next day our Fien said, as she came out of the cowshed with the milk:

'Root, one of these days you should take our Lis to the Twister's bull.' Then that desire began thrashing about once more. I had promised never to set foot in there again, and now my own wife was urging me on to do it. If I fall now, it's no longer my fault, I told myself. And I forgot the priest's beautiful sermon and the stars of my wedding night. The following day, early in the morning, I took our cow to the Twister's bull. The maid was home alone. That filled my legs with lead and unleashed a storm in my heart. She helped the bull cover the cow. She fired me up with her words and passionate laughter. I became as if blind. We put the bull in its stall. In the stall doorway I grabbed her in the loins. She throws her arms around my neck and she falls, and I fall with her.

Falling is easy, but getting up! Bang! The bull is suddenly outside. The stupid hussy hadn't tied him up and I was too blinded to notice. The bull outside! And he raced head first out of the yard and into the fields. God in heaven! I shall never forget it. Even now when I think about it, I almost collapse. We followed it, or rather I followed it alone, because the maid was running about like a madwoman, screaming and taking a different direction with her arms flailing. The bull galloped this way and that, the clods of earth flew into the air. There was no question of catching him. I shouted, swore, prayed. Over there by the brook were children. Mine! The bull made a beeline for them. Then I was so horrified I covered my face with my hands, and fell to my knees.

I could not, I dared not look up. I knelt:

'God never again, never again. I'd rather cut my throat, help me, Your poor Root.'

I hear voices, shouting, my name: 'Root! Root!' See, Holy God! The Oxhead, who was just coming on the scene, had seen the danger and risking his own life had made the bull change direction!

On the path the bull was now playing ball with Bel Salamander's goat. That is, the bull in his rage threw the creature in the air about six times with his horns, and mashed it into a dish rag with his horns and feet.

At the same time farmers had come running from all directions, including the Twister, who was able to bring the bull under control and lead it away.

'How did it happen, Root?'

'How? Well… it suddenly broke free of me. It was as if the devil had a hand in it…'

I dared not say: God. I didn't dare take your name in vain, O Lord, but I let loose a whole string of curses.

The maid never came back. She had gone straight home, three hours away. One of her brothers came to collect her clothes the following day. 'She got a fright,' he said. Just as long as she didn't get anything else, I thought to myself.

The affair weighed long and painfully on my mind. I no longer dared look our Fien in the eye. If the question of sexual relations came up, I quietly

32

rejected it. It seemed to me that everyone could read my sins in my face.

At night I dreamed that the Oxhead had horns and was the bull.

I didn't dare mention it to anyone and yet I had to speak about it.

My heart was full. If I was alone with the children, I told them about the bull and always ended with a nice lesson:

'Yes, kids, it was your guardian angel that called Oxhead into the fields. You must always pray for that angel and always be good, otherwise he'll desert you.'

Once one of those snotty-nosed kids, the blind girl, asked you:

'Weren't you good then, Dad?'

'Why?'

'Because your guardian angel left you in the lurch.'

'How?'

'Because you couldn't hold the bull any longer, Dad.'

I was left blinking. If I talked about it later, and they had to ask me, I left out the lesson of the guardian angel.

God pulled the bull towards my children for my punishment. My promise saved them. I'd rather cut my throat. Thank God! You who work in such curious ways. Everything comes from you and through you. I suddenly felt and saw that then deep in my heart. Now I know that You count and arrange the seeds that we throw in whole handfuls into the furrows. So many for the birds and so many for the farmer. Now

I know that good and bad weather depends on our actions. I shall listen to you! No one but You and me, O Lord, knows that the knife, ground and whetted, is ready in grey paper in the food chest.

Two things continued to weigh heavily on my liver. How the maid was doing, and the fact that I had to confess at Easter. In anticipation I stored up conscience and grief, hoping to be a different father. Yet that wasn't my intention. Oh, what's done is done, and regret is always too late. Though this going to confession was still to come and I could fix it. But how?

It is simply not possible that I should say to our good friend the priest: I and that maid... That's impossible. He certainly won't let the cat out of the bag, he's a clergyman standing between us and God. But after all, he's a human being as well, who will see me very differently when he crosses our threshold. You can no longer speak freely about someone else, without him looking at you and your reading in his look: consider yourself. Yet I must confess everything to him. A bad confession then? I'd rather... not be dead, but rather not confess. It could keep me awake at night. What if I say to him: I forgot my marriage vows. The he will say: how many times my son. And if I then say twelve times more or less, he will definitely not ask for an explanation, he also has his time to consider. But if I say once, father, then he'll want to know all the details, and that's precisely what I want to avoid... 'What are you thinking about this time, Root, you look so bewildered?' asks my wife.

'About nothing, about the grain, I mean about the eggs.'

I was thinking about hell.

What if I told everything to our Fien, honestly, quite frankly. What a consolation she could be to me. A woman can overlook so much, they have something so mild about them. See her with the children, when she prays in church and asks for happiness and blessing she pushes the children to the front; if there is thunder and lightning, she stands in front of the children to take the blow. As she is for the children, so she is for me. And now my heart does not know which way to turn from fear, could she not lighten it? You don't know our Fien!

Once in bed I hold her tight.

'Fien, I have to tell you something.'

'Yes, Root...'

But I can't get it off my chest. To be seen as a sinner all your life, by your own wife? Even despite all the forgiveness, consolation and oblivion, no, no, no. Now she has a good opinion of me, that gives her calm and happiness, and hence me as well. After my death she has to be able to say to the children:

'Your father was a model man.' That is also a legacy.

'Yes, Root?'

'I wish I were dead, Fien.'

'Root, Root, don't torture me with death,' she cried.

'I wish I were dead, Fien, that means if you die, I'll die too, I love you so much...'

The fear evaporated, and we loved each other.

Isn't it better like that?

But I couldn't get rid of my burden. Easter was approaching. It was as if I had to walk through a great fire. Usually, I went to confession on Palm Sunday. Now even Easter itself was passing by too.

'I'm going with the millers, on the last day,' I said to our Fien.

Putting it off, putting it off and still I had to go through with it.

In the week I go and drink a pint in 'The Half Moon' to strengthen my spirit and to refresh my heart. There stands the Turnip and the husband of Jef Broes's Mie. And I hear them say (to think I had to come in just at that point!...) that the maid had gone crazy and had had a child. I was so embarrassed I stuck my nose in my glass of beer. Fathering a child on another woman! For my whole life a ball and chain on my soul. I sat nailed to my seat.

You bad person! You bad person! I reproached my-self, you're not worthy to live. But at the same time I was glad that the maid, now she was mad, wouldn't tell any stories. I got up to go, but then I hear the husband of Jef Broes's Miesay to the Turnip: 'You've got something to do with this, Turnip.'

'We'll let God and the miller decide that, Jef,' said the Turnip. 'I went along once, but there's the Dox and the Oxhead, and I can name at least ten who came after me.'

Ha, what I fool I am! I thought, can't you add up anymore then? My business was six months ago, in October!

And I began to laugh and laugh. Have a pint on me, men, and another. Ha, that was a relief! Or half of one, that confessional burden had to be lifted too. Three more days and Easter would be over. If a farmer doesn't celebrate Easter, there's a chance his carrots will turn into turnips. At night, when I lie awake, a good idea comes into my head. To go to town, to another priest to confess; they won't know me there!

No sooner said than done.

'Fien, I'm going to town for seed.' I went to confession with the Jesuits.

'How many times?' asked the father.

'Once, more or less,' I said, flustered.

'Right, and don't do it again, my friend.'

That friar may never have had a confessant who made his act of contrition so sincerely.

An hour later I sat in the confessional of my priest telling him about my minor sins… adding a drop of water to the milk, getting rather angry on one occasion, and so on.

Still the same good person, he'll have thought.

Ha! It was a beautiful Low Sunday. With my spirit purified, in my white shirtsleeves with the wind playing through them, with a cigar planted on my dogtooth, I walked proudly round the field. My happiness gave praise to God!

Yes, those Sundays are of great importance to us farmers, not that we rest from our work, but we rest in order to begin again. To mass in the morning, then a few pints, fat meat on the table, an hour sitting at our ease, or taking a nap on the verge of the road, playing some bowls and then going for a walk on your own, across the brook, through woods and fields. Everything is Sunday-like, quieter, softer, even the chickens are aware of it and the animals in the meadow.

And evening comes sweetly, you sit at the door. Always looking at the field, the eternal field in which you are rooted. The wife is out in the neighbourhood and the children are in the village, I'm sure. And then you fetch your bugle. I used to be in the band, but the band disintegrated because of a row between the priest and the brewer. I still know a polka from it and I play that. It sounds curious across all those silent distances. If I stop playing for a second, I hear a piece of it coming from the woods. The cow observes you from the cowshed, the pig sticks its snout out of its sty. And what's a man like? Vain, and like a child. Because the cow and the pig are listening you play better than usual, with vibrato and tremolos.

A farmer doesn't have much happiness, but those are hours like eggs.

You're happy to be resting, but also happy that tomorrow you can stand there in your sweaty trousers again and go and plough the field. You can already smell the soil that rolls open. It smells of medicines. And I go and do that and forget to go on playing.

God, let there be plenty of fields up in Your heaven, because what else am to do with my hands? The wife comes home, she lights the lamp and I go and have a look, that is I go and drink beer, to be happy, mighty, holy and everything again. Why doesn't it work without beer? Happiness isn't just thrown into your lap, it says in books, you have to do something for it… if only drink beer.

Each time the priest comes or we meet each other, it gives me renewed pleasure that I fooled the man, so well, with that confession.

But one morning when I'm planting cauliflowers, and we are talking about a murder in another village, he says: 'Yes, Root my lad, who would ever have thought it of that man? From that you can see that all of us, I as well as you, can be a murderer or a great sinner tomorrow, if we forget that God is in us. The best sheep of Our Dear Lord can go astray. But it's some consolation that, when God breaks through in us, the greatest murderer and sinner can become a saint. Look at St. Augustine, the liberties he took with women, and St. Paul who killed the first Christians like flies in October. And do we reproach the saint with that? What is it Root?… you're trembling… a little unwell? Did you have pint too many yesterday?'

But I lie with my face in his hands, sobbing, and I tell him everything, about the confession and that girl and that bull and my struggle. His beautiful soul, which burned in his words, opened my heart.

I lay awake many nights, trying to work out how to make confession in a cunning way, and now I shout it at him frankly in his face! In the open field.

'Life is no laughing matter,' he said, 'but now I have to laugh, Root, because you trust me more out of the confessional than in it. Root, lad, give me five!'

That was the beginning of our great friendship.

III

ONE baby in its cradle, another in its coffin. In the morning I go to the cemetery with the neighbours' children to bury my child. In the afternoon I hold a different child over the font with the midwife.

In the morning the priest shook my hand:

'Courage, Root,' he said. In the afternoon he shook hands with me again. 'Congratulations, Root,' he said, 'where God strikes, He also soothes.'

You just have to accept this because the priest says so. I accept it. But all that striking and soothing gets so mixed up and confuses you so, that you'd almost say thank you if they punched you in the face.

In the long run a man says to the King on high: 'Do what You want, it's Your responsibility.'

I've sworn a lot in my life, but never cursed. I've occasionally pulled a sour face at God, and forgotten him too, but never raised my fist at him. I do my Christian duties as well as I can, I make the sign of the cross on time, go to mass on Sundays, regularly celebrate Easter, and when there's a fair I, with the Oxhead, carry the statue of St. Anthony with his pig in the procession. You should see me, with white gloves, with my eyes downcast and my heart sometimes raised to God. How at the most beautiful moments a man can think of the most stupid things.

But our priest knows very well how fragile human beings are; he relieves us of the worries of faith.

You don't have to pray all day,' he says, 'all you must do is dedicate your work to God at the start of the day, and in that way your work will be praying.'

If that's true my life is one great prayer!

That prayer begins every year, roundabout Candlemas. Then the snow falls on a hot stone. God stretches the sky and it stays light longer.

We plough the field, the lovely black greasy soil. We fill it full of cowshed dung to refresh it, make it full of life and ready for our purposes. We plough again to give each handful of earth its due. God pours his bottles of water on top, breathes some early sun over it, and now the soil is saturated, full of sap and ready to receive the seed and its residue. In the meantime, because from now on we have no time to sit down, we dig the garden over, lay out beds, sections and plots.

The caterpillars' nests are burnt, the hedges pruned, the beehives brushed with lime and cow dung. And according to the waning and waxing of the moon we sow and plant: the onions, the leeks, the radishes, the savoy cabbages.

You plant cauliflower when the moon is on the wane, you sow carrots when there's not a breath of wind, with a full March moon, and parsley on a Tuesday.

Oh, the moon is as mysterious as a cat. It creeps through the night and pours its enchantment over everything, which is in part a blessing and in part poison.

I always try to stay on good terms with the moon, you have to get to know it. The dogs know it too. I will never look at its mysterious cat's head for too long. The fact that our Amelieken was born blind is the fault of the moon. At the time when our Fien was still carrying the child, there was an eclipse of the moon. The neighbours all stood watching it. A heavy disc crept across the full moon. One person said this, the other that: bad for the corn, bad for the butter. Bel Salamander comes past.

'Are you crazy?' she shouted to our Fien, 'standing there watching it! The next thing the child will have a swollen head.'

Our Fien covered her eyes with her hands and went into the house. Our Amelieken was born blind. You simply can't convince our Fien that it's the fault of the moon.

'It's God who willed it so,' she says.

And so we almost dragged God out of heaven to give that child a ray of light. The more light we lit, the darker it became for her. We tried everything, pilgrimages and medicines. I even, like Tobias, as I'd read in the holy story, rubbed the gall of a fish on her eyes!

Oh no, they won't write any holy story about Root. She remained blind.

At the beginning, like cat and mouse, we waited for a miracle, but eventually you resign yourself. The child too. She plays and sings. You get used to everything, it's just when she sometimes says: 'I'd really like to see our Mum and Dad,' that you again raise your arms in the air in lamentation.

I also listen to the moon when planting potatoes. That's around Eastertime. The soil is ready but potatoes like to grow in a pool of cess. We get the cess at night from the toilets in town and each potato is given a ladleful, almost a soup tureen. That gives it courage. What we give to people as beautiful vegetables, we get back as cess to produce fresh vegetables. I like that.

I don't allow chemicals in my house. I don't want to poke God's eyes out. He gives us rain, dew and the dung of animals and people. Nature not hormones! And if my potatoes turn out a little smaller than those of the Oxhead, I've pulled them out of the ground without tricks and without poison. That's a pleasure, and I know they're better, healthier and with more heart. I laugh at their chemicals.

The days open clear and wide, the sun sucks everything upwards. Including what's bad, and now it's a constant fight against weeds: weeding, digging up, planting and replanting and forever crawling. We put the stakes on the peas, dig new furrows, plant and replant and spy and feel for asparagus. Not a moment is lost, neither in the yard nor in the field. Our Fien with her headaches, with a new child at the breast, blind Amelieken on her apron strings, makes butter, milks, cooks and looks after people and beasts. The animals are given the fresh-cut corn, the clover is in the manger and the chickens lay as if for their pleasure.

Yet again our hearts are filled with worry and pleasure. The hay grass is high, thick and lush, but it's full of slugs. Crash, a dark cloud comes from across the Nete and hail pounds the crops into pulp. The teeth of the new moon gleam like crystal. God strews the dew in clear handfuls and the men adore that. You see the corn growing. But then the ice saints come, they wipe their feet on our pleasure and freeze the young shoots. No cherries for those men now! The crosses wend their way through the fields, I follow them. Now the misery runs out of the sky and those up there start to bask in the sun. We lift the new potatoes, pick berries and peas and pull up the young carrots. Twice a week I drive at night to the early morning market, but the prices are going down year by year. Everyone wants to attend the market, and the buyers agree between themselves to offer as little as possible. We have to sell our quality crops for a song. They enjoy cheating a peasant farmer, and they laugh at you behind your back. But I cheat them too: I put the nicest vegetables and eggs on top.

The sun pours down all it can, and with our Amelieken on my back, I go on foot to Scherpenheuvel, seven hours away. You feel it in your bones for two days afterwards, but work calls, and you mustn't laze about!

And although we've not rested and given it all we've got, it's nothing compared with what's about to come. One morning all of us are up mowing before dawn. First we are dripping with dew, then with sweat. My almanac forecasts rain, yesterday the frogs croaked at the moon, so we must go on working to catch the last glimmer of light. The following day, back to the grind. We arrange for twenty-four eggs to be taken to the Sisters of Mercy to keep the rain off. The sun bites, pricks, bakes me till I'm a year older, but the hay dries, and that means everything. Provided the animals eat well!

A farmer works more for his animals than for himself. They're what oats and clover grow for, the beets, the turnips, the hay—we work at it day and night. They get the best, everything they like, and they live like burgomasters in the meadow and grow bulky and fat. We eat frugally and stay thin and poor. But there you have the farmer's trade. You complain bitterly, but none of you changes his trade. That's the holy compulsion from on high. God needs His contingent of farmers.

Before you can say Jack Robinson, there's no stopping it, the soil is ready for sowing the turnips and beets, and the empty spaces that are created are ploughed again and soaked with dung and liquid manure.

God rattles the clouds, opens the cloud sluices and hurls thunderbolts into the world. We cringe, keep our ears pricked for the cracks and promise always to be good. We get through it unscathed. There is the rainbow, the corn still stands straight, so do we, and we've forgotten our promises. The rod no longer threatens our backsides!

Ha! If only there were more onions. Nothing counts. Only onions. There's a huge demand for onions. The priest said it (how does he know?): 'Plant more onions.' Next year I'll plant a whole bunch of onions. And when the cherries have been picked, we crown our work by harvesting the corn. The heat has beaten down for days and days, the corn ripens day and night, it's ready for cutting, dry and crispy. The palms that we planted at the four corners at Easter have given their blessing. They say that an angel stands on watch by each corn stalk. You watched well, angels! But mind your lovely toes, get out of the way, for we bend and wield the pickaxe until tomorrow we can no longer stand straight!

The sky's helmet is a single flame, which seems to pour boiling water over us. The corn falls under the pickaxe, it falls, it falls constantly, and we wish we were corn ourselves so we could fall too, could lie, rest for all eternity, amen. The work is so wretched, the drive to finish it is so hectic. You burn, you glow. The blisters surround your palms and you sometimes look round to see whether you haven't melted to a puddle. The frail lady from the chateau, who will eat corn bread thanks to our sweat, comes driving by in an open carriage with a parasol. She likes *la vie champêtre* and wants to cheer us up with her presence. But to have my revenge I start singing and the others join in: 'I and fat boy Dick went out corn to pick, but the corn was not yet ripe and fat boy got a pipe.'

Now I know she feels even more unhappy than us. When the corn is put up in sheaves it is time for the village fair. Then I gargle with a glass of gin, and sit in our rainwater butt for a quarter of an hour, in order to open up all the blocked holes in my body. I take part in the procession and that evening I go for a pint with our Fien, and give her a twirl in the dance tent. Usually our Fransoo, who's a monk with the barefoot friars in Dendermonde, comes on Monday. There's a lot left over from the day before. The lad can go on eating and he doesn't waste anything. He amuses the children with little pictures, medals and stories about angels and Our Lady. He tries to comfort me in our adversity by talking about Our Dear Lord, but I enjoy contradicting him and making him angry. I don't mean to, but it goes back to when we were little. Apart from that it's difficult to take moral lessons from one's own brother, and one who's much younger. But he doesn't get angry, there's no way you can wipe that happy smile off his face. And imagine that he used to be a real fidget! In a monastery they take the barbed wire out of a man's heart. Could they do that with me too?

On Tuesday we both went, Fransoo and me, to visit our crazy brother.

Even from when he was small, he had a screw loose. Still, he learned well at school and could soon read and write, but he wasn't fit for work, he dreamt the whole time. He was given a hard time by our dad, but it made no difference.

He usually strolled through the woods by himself and when he came home he would start fibbing. He had seen a snake, a giant or a lady with a crown, who was driving through the wood in a carriage. He could tell stories in such a way that you had to believe them. If we believed him he would laugh at us. If we didn't believe him, he flew into a rage. Our dad apprenticed him to the wheelwright, then to the blacksmith, and then he joined us on the farm again. Jack of all trades and master of none. Once, he was eighteen at the time, he came home with the nail, so he said, with which they had nailed Our Dear Lord's right hand to the cross. He had been given it by a hermit. It was an ordinary horseshoe-nail, slightly bent at the end. A few weeks later the bishop came for confirmation. And goodness me if he doesn't go up to the bishop and say: 'That is the nail from Our Dear Lord's cross, if you please.' The bishop, to get rid of him, said: 'Right friend, keep it with you for a while.'

And from then on the madness become really intense. For whole days on end he talked to God and everyone about that holy nail. Those who did not think he was right, received blows. We had to send him to the asylum at Geel. There everyone thought he was right. Yes, he still knows us very well. He's able to recall everything about the past. It's just that stupid story of the nail that can't be eradicated from his thoughts. From morn till night he stands outside the town hall of Geel, with the nail in his hand. 'Monsignor lives in there,' he says, 'soon he'll come to fetch Our Dear Lord's nail.'

The sucker has been standing there for years, day after day, minute by minute, in the rain and hail, snow and heat, patiently, without sighing or groaning, with that nail, waiting for the bishop.

I'm always glad when I've left Geel; it's crawling with lunatics, one is Our Lady, the other goes 'puff,

puff', like a train; another thinks he's Napoleon. If I should have to stay there any longer there's a chance I'd join in the game. And apart from that, I'm always afraid that a maid would come and shout: 'The bull's loose! The bull's loose!'

Yes, my sins go on haunting me, and remorse is not enough to blot them out. After all, it's my fault that that maid went mad and knowing that is a dark stain on my life. That's how someone goes mad. Fortunately, there's my field, which always ploughs those worries under.

Back home our Fransoo goes round the farms with his begging sack. With the money he has assembled for the love of God, for his poor little monastery, I could pay half a year's rent.

'A nice trade, being a Franciscan,' I say, in order to tease him. But he gives me such a friendly smile that I chip in two silver five-franc pieces.

The corn is in. The potatoes are coming out. While you plough to prepare the soil for the winter corn, the first leaves start to fall. Then it's also time to pull up the turnips. It's already growing dark early, every day God closes his curtain more and more. When the dry potato tops burn in the fields in the evening, you're right to think Mr Winter is coming. We get fog and rain and we plough, fertilise and harrow, sow the oats and the wheat.

All Saints, All Souls. The mourning bells toll in the fog. It smells of dead leaves. Our Fien bakes cakes and at the same time we pray for the pious souls. For all the deceased of family and friends, even for our Polleken, even though we know he's an angel in heaven. In particular for my little grandmother. She could not die! She lay in her death agony for two days, and was constantly singing the song of Sir Halewijn. When we were little she had often told us about Halewijn, who lured women with his beautiful songs and then cut off their heads. But now there was a maiden who was too clever for him and herself cut off his head. And the head cried: 'Go into the corn and blow on the horn.' But she did not go into the corn, she rode home with the head, and held a banquet and put the head on the table. When she told us that our hair stood on end with fright, and now that song was playing in her head. She kept saying: 'I won't go into the corn, I won't blow on the horn. I'll run away, I'll run away. Sir Halewijn will ride after me on horseback, without a head, without a head, and shoot arrows, but won't hit me.'

She thrashed about with her arms and legs, terror was in her eyes, streams of sweat ran over the wrinkles in her face. Terrible to behold. I still remember it so well; outside the storm howled and knocked the stones out of the chimney breast. 'There he is, there he is,' she cried again, but he won't catch me, I'll swim across the Nete, I'll run through the woods, children pray, pray, his arrows miss, ha,ha,ha!' The priest tried to calm her. It worked for a minute, then the chase began again. She gasped, sweated, was exhausted by all that imaginary running, but each time terror forced her to flee.

Towards the evening of the second day, when the last thread of flesh had been consumed, she cried out happily: 'Damn, it isn't Sir Halewijn! Now he has a head, but it's the face of Our Dear Lord! How beautiful, how beautiful. If only I'd known!... Jesus is chasing after my soul... oh lovely huntsman, shoot...'

She bared her scrawny breast: 'Shoot! Shoot!' she cried.

'Ah, a hit... How sweet, how sweet!' Then she collapsed, and died with beautiful contentment around her mouth.

'That's no laughing matter, to die like that,' said the priest pensively, 'there's something holy about it.'

Now the dark days come, the rain lashes against the window panes and in the wild rain we pull up the beets, and put the celery, the leeks and potatoes in their holes. It's the time of colds.

The days open and close, they're too short to finish the work in the cowshed and the barn. We kill our pig, and heaven knows how he knows, but the priest arrives right on time. He sings the praises of the pig.

'Ha!' he says, 'a cutlet of that in the pan, with a stump of cabbage, that's good eating!' or: 'A slice of ham wound round an endive and popped in the oven with a cheese sauce!'

I ask him straight out: 'Well, father, you who are so learned and know Latin, do you know the difference between the death of this pig and the death of Our Dear Lord?'

'No, Root, lad,' he says.

'Well,' I say, 'Our Dear Lord died for everyone, and this pig only for me.'

'I have to recite my breviary,' he says and with that he is gone. But the next day when the pig has thawed, our children carry half a basket of cutlets, roast meat and black pudding to his house and come back with seven bottles of white and red wine! We'll keep those till New Year! At the chateau that's the one day they won't be drinking wine!

It snows, it freezes, there are storms. Now we thresh and lay in stocks of manure, seed and firewood.

The evenings last too long but it's a nice time for poaching.

I know where the hares and the pheasants are and can sell them to the poulterer in town. Or else I carve some wooden toys for the children by the fire. For years I've been working on a stable of Bethlehem. I already have lots of figures: a St, Joseph, Mary and the baby. Every year a king or a shepherd is added. The youngest among them are pleased with them, and the eldest laugh at them. Now I've made the ass, and his head nods 'yes', much to the delight of the children Again the eldest ones laugh...: Dad, that must be the camel with which Our Dear Lord terrified the devils in limbo?'

Our children go carol-singing in the village with a star I've made.

New Year is here. One by one we carefully taste the wine. We pull sour faces, but everyone says: 'Oh, that's nice.' I say so too, but soon I go and drink a healthy pint of rich barley brew in the neighbourhood!'

The year is over. Now it's time to collect everything from nooks and crannies, from the stocking and from under the flat stone. Everything is totted up, and you are allowed to take that lovely money, for which you've sweated blood, back to the chateau with a smile on your face. The frail lady complains bitterly and threatens to lock you up, as she has to eat into her capital and can't live on the interest!...

Well, now God has lent a helping hand! You've lived frugally, you've sold your milk, butter and eggs, and the sweet honey. You yourself spread the fat from fried bacon on your bread and slurped blue buttermilk porridge! For whom have you worked, sweated, toiled and stood for a year in the sludge?

Our Fien needs a new hooded cloak, my toes are poking through my shoes, the children don't have proper trousers to wear. Good that the priest brings some discarded clothes from his brother.

And onions are selling at one franc a kilo. If only we'd planted onions. Next year one, no, three beds of onions! Don't breathe a word to anyone about it.

We plant lots of onions, but so does everyone, the Oxhead and the others. When the season comes, they'll pelt you with onions.

So it goes, year in, year out. In the books you can read that farmers grow rich, but paper is long-suffering.

They won't break us. Poverty is no shame. We've been given hands to use them. I do what I can and if it doesn't pay enough, still I shan't hold it against Our Dear Lord. I don't ask for riches. What would I do with a chateau, if there was no dung heap outside the door and chickens didn't thrive in the house? I ask for our daily bread and good health. I'll provide the rest. Because my main pleasure in life is to work in my field. To see what I myself have planted and sown grow and blossom. It's my heaven on earth, my field.

God, stick your finger in my heart and you can rest assured you'll find, apart from a few tadpoles, nothing but gratitude.

IV

SNOW and dark winter, and I'm carving a great big Christ on the Cross. Who for? What for? For my own pleasure? Or because a man starts to resemble Our Dear Lord somewhat through all his misery?

'It's also a form of prayer,' says the priest, who is just frightened that the statue will be too ugly for words.

But I'm saving the face till last, till next winter. First I'll carve his hands and feet. I've made an impression of my hands in clay and now I'm carving them.

'Those hands and feet will be too big for the rest,' says our Fien, much to my alarm. 'You're giant of a fellow, Root, and this Jesus is only as big as our little Gerard.'

'That's nothing. I'll saw the Jesus in two, and insert another piece. Let me get on with it, and as long as you can see it's a Jesus, I'll be happy.'

Yes, it certainly is a form of prayer, for sometimes in the midst of my fumbling about I survey those hands and feet. I imagine it to myself. Ow! The hammer shoots flames through my hands and feet. The little bones splinter and crack like pipe stems. The pains shoot all through my body. I close my fingers because of the terrible pain; the hammer smashes the tips of my fingers, the fingernails split. The left foot placed on the right foot is crushed into a bloody mess, so that the nail, which is too short, can be driven deep into the wood.

I can see and feel myself hanging on a stake. My hands are torn, my feet swell up as blue as blisters.

I can sometimes imagine it so vividly that when I get up I'm limping. Yes, Jesus must have suffered infinitely. It's because of that that you feel it so acutely.

And you're consoled somewhat by your own way of the cross through life. A little. For although the latter is just a feather compared with a thousand kilos of lead, still it is so hard to bear that you can't understand how someone's heart doesn't break under the weight.

It all begins so beautifully. When you go courting and get married it's as if the world was made especially for the two of you. Fresh with dew, full of fragrant flowers. But you're no sooner in this land of promise than the blisters start to rise, and you are soon in misery. With work, with illnesses and with poverty. Each time you think: it can't get any worse, the storm's passed, and once it's passed everything will go smoothly again. But there's no end to it, the future's dark, moments come when one longs, like You, O Lord, to be able to say: It is finished…

I have known plenty of misery, with my field, with illness, death, the evil hand, but the worst thing is conflict with one's children. If you're unlucky with them! I've had my share of this, and now I understand so well, O Lord, why you let yourself be crucified to save your children.

Oh, it's such a strange business with children!

To start with you gave them all that was in your power. The best of you is in them, your blood, your soul, your life. They're a part of you. Their happiness is yours, their sorrow cuts deeper into you than into them. You warm their life with your heart. And behold, one day you see that they're fundamentally your fiercest enemies. Yes, they still love you as a person. They'll fight for you at the cost of a few holes in the head, and when you lie dying they'll be downcast. But their heart is no longer yours, nor their will, their desire, the life that stirs in their core, you've been skittled out of it.

You can't stand it! You want to share joy and sorrow with them. No, you're not even allowed to see into their hearts anymore. I was a child with the children, in their play and their lives. I want to stay a child with them, but they become people and keep you separate as a burden. Despite all that you still love them all passionately. One child is no better than another in that way. And to have your revenge, you wish: Wait, you'll be a father or mother one day, and you'll have the same problem. Bah! You don't need to wish. It will find its own way into the mix. But if on top of that they turn out bad! First they tread on your toes and afterwards on your heart. Then one cringes with dismay.

Why didn't You let them choke in the cradle, O Lord! Why didn't You make them into angels? Forgive those words, O Lord, it's just a manner of speaking.

But must I be punished in my children? If it please you, no! Crucify me, break my bones, let my field be a prey to weeds and vermin, but keep Your hands off my children!

You have made me the shepherd of twelve children, you have taken four away from me, and each time, although I grumbled, and was not happy about it, I bowed my head. And if you need any more, just come and get them. But those you allow me to keep, let them not be the bane of our life. I will give up all the others, but bring our Fons back to the path of righteousness. For one stray sheep the good shepherd abandoned the whole flock, it says in Your books. Who are You saying that to?

Our Fons, the survivor of the twins, had a short-tempered and stubborn nature, oh, it takes all sorts. Poor consolation. But circumstances brought out all the bad in him.

He had started courting a girl from the Plattekeeshoek, a huddle of poor houses behind the village, where all the riffraff gathered. She was just like a Bohemian, with greasy black hair and eyes like coals. Beautiful figure, but not for a farmer's boy, something for an itinerant harmonica player, a really, low, outspoken creature, a bawdy wench.

He took enough knocks because of it. Our Fien tried sweetness. Then he said, 'You did what you wanted, and so will I.'

What did I really care who he married, just so long as your child was happy in the future. But what if you feel in your bones that a woman like that will bring him nothing but misery?

One time, when I had seen him with that puss, and had hidden his Sunday things and his watch, he went off with lots of threats. I laughed, but at night he was still not back. Our Fien was terribly upset, frightened and suspicious and I was reproached for having hit him too hard: 'He's probably drowned. I just hope he doesn't have one of his funny moods.' She groaned. She lit a candle for Our Lady. It wasn't the first. Kilos of candles had gone up in smoke. The following morning he was still not there. I had to go and look for him. On the way I heard he had spent the night with his she-cat. He had all his clothes fetched and informed us that he was not coming home anymore, and was going to work in Antwerp harbour.

That's when you see what a mother is. The woman's grief cut me to the quick: I was burning with rage, because harvest time was approaching and then you're always short-handed. He knew that, that was his Judas's game.

'Leave him where he is, we'll show him who's strongest, him or me.'

But if a woman, a mother like our Fien is standing beside you, a father is helpless. Whole days of tears, praying, pleading eyes and pleading hands. Unbearable, and the outcome was that I gave our Fien permission to bring him back, with the promise that he could continue to court that girl. And then he comes back home, with such a poisonous smile on his lips that it drove you up the wall. And on top of that you had to keep silent. It's as if they were breaking your ribs on a lathe.

O Lord, I thank you for gin, which makes me see life as more beautiful, and stops me from murdering my own flesh and blood.

Now he went about openly in my sight with that witch. That was up to him. Whoever burns his melon, must take the consequences, I say. But I don't mean it. You can't stand it, and you get a constant pain in your heart, and you sometimes stand in front of the mirror to see whether you can't read the grief in your eyes.

You hope. He's still young, he can still leave her, because he still had to enter the ballot for military service.

Our Fien, Bel Salamander and Aloiske give him advice and teach him little prayers to ensure one misses the ballot. Our Fien makes paper roses and ribbons for his hat, and gives him a crucifix too. Of course, he is chosen in the ballot. Just my luck. If a tile falls off the roof, rest assured it'll fall on my head. The *petit cousin* of the frail lady from the chateau also loses out, with an even lower number than our Fons. No harm done, they deposited sixteen hundred francs, they're buying themselves out! *Petit cousin*, whom they call Coco, can stay home and my son can spend three years learning how to shoot and kill people.

He'll have to go to Wallonia, to Arlon.

Get moving, engine-driver! And he who had never travelled in a train! Our Fien was of course very sad about it and so was I. A good pair of hands gone, and no longer being able to see each other. But from one point of view I thought it was a stroke of luck. In three years a lot of water flows under the bridge, and meanwhile he may forget that sweetheart. Let's hope so. But with Root luck never lasts long. A month later, I can still see how our Fien collapsed, our Fons's black lover came to tell she was about to become a mother. I could have beaten her to a pulp. I had to get away, away quickly, because if I let a harsh word fall, I knew in advance that the pair of lovers would answer triumphantly: 'It was the same with you!' And I didn't want our Fien to be humiliated like that.

When the time came for him to leave for those distant parts, the whole house wept, except for me. I was still hopeful that everything would turn out as we wanted, I drove him with his sweetheart to the station. She hung round his neck like a drowning person clinging to the mast. He almost missed his train she made such a fuss. When I drove her back home with me, she came and sat close to me on the seat, bawling all the while. Sobbing, she laid her black head on my shoulder and gripped my arm tight. I'm not used to a soppy female like that. Was it playacting? Real grief? Or what? She pushed herself right up against me. She put her arm round my shoulders, I felt her soft body, her breasts against my arm. Suddenly I understood why our Fons was such a slave to her. A beautiful she-devil! My blood was dancing, and sometimes I saw nothing but white before my eyes. But I didn't stir. I kept as stiff as a board, didn't say a word, and gradually I felt like knocking her off the cart with my fist, or else wrapping my arms round her and rolling into the cart together with her. I thought of the bull, of Fons's claim on her. But it wouldn't be long before

Root was lying down with her! I couldn't resist. I was so frenzied and nervous that I used the whip on my horse and started driving, driving. I wanted to drive my thoughts and desires into the ground. How no accidents happened, I still don't know.

At the mill I suddenly stopped.

'Just get off here, I've got to see the Twister.'

I really did go to see the Twister, I didn't want to lie.

'You're so pale, Root,' he said.

'From taking our Fons to the train, Twister.'

He gave me a gin to bring me round.

But now she came to ours almost every day, asking for news and telling us things about our Fons. Now she was like a lamb, acted soft and bashful, and one word was no louder than the other. Was that incident in the cart real grief after all? I avoided her. And yet I sometimes stood and spied on her though the gap in the door. For days after I felt the spot where she had stroked my arm with her body like a warm glow.

I hated her, was afraid of her, but I found it curious behaviour that I didn't say a word, not one word, to our Fien about the cart business.

In any case I had a look in the drawer to see if the knife was still there, and still as sharp as ever.

Fons's sweetheart found favour with our Fien. She thought her a handy and reasonable girl, who would later make Fons a good wife. She helped with the sewing, darned socks or crocheted a bedspread for later. In the winter the child was born. Our Fien went to help her and paid for the coffee and currant cakes out of her own pocket and saw to the baby basket. Now the baby was there we saw less of her, and when Fons came home on leave, every three months, he naturally spent his days with her. But gradually things started to go wrong. She came and complained that he wrote so little. When he came home on leave, she had to come and pick him up at our place, and he did not stay with her for so long. They argued a lot.

There was a snag. I wished there would be a whole lot. Our Fien did not: 'There's the baby,' she said, 'our Fons must do his duty. And we must save up so that when he leaves the army next year, he can quickly marry her.'

Meanwhile our Sus succeeded in avoiding the ballot and was going out with a model farm girl, fresh and blushing, handy, serious and money saved. She had hands like cushions and could milk so well that you could listen to it like a brass band.

Not everything has to be a setback. They'll marry next year on 1 October.

The more I see of that girl at our place, the angrier I get with our Fons's she-cat. Once she came to ask for news. She hadn't had a word in reply from him for a month. And in the letters he wrote to us, there was no question any more of 'Give my regards to Frisine.' He behaved as if Frisine didn't exist. Our Sus wrote him a long letter, dictated by our Fien. The answer was that he had no time and needed money.

He has to come on leave. But no sign of our Fons. Now our Fien told me to dictate an angry letter, as if my words written down by Sus would have more effect than hers. Just as I was dictating, Frisine comes in crying with a letter. A letter from a friend—our Fons had yet again not come home on leave—telling her that Fons is going out with a woman from a disreputable pub, who had once been a dancer in the theatre in Brussels, and is at least ten years older than he is.

Now the priest had to write the letter. It was beautiful letter, enough to turn someone's heart upside down.

His answer was that he would make love to whoever he wanted, and it was none of the priest's business, and anyway, was the child his?

We kept anxiously silent about that letter with other people. But Frisine must have heard something similar from that friend, because two days after the fair she comes storming in with a lot of rumpus, and sets the baby on the table with a bang. 'If this child isn't his then it's not mine either.' And with that she swept out of the door.

We were left literally holding the baby! More angry at the gesture than at the child. Because we loved Liesken and she often came to us for a day or two to play. O she was so fond of Grandad and Grannie! Our Fien was happy about it. Now she knew that the child would be well looked after and have what it needed, much better than in the Plattekeeshoek. She was soon close to my heart. It was a consolation to me to be once again a child with a child, and to regain what I had lost in the others. We saw no more of that rotten mother, and our Fons too waffled and asked for money, avoiding the issue. What will become of the lad?

Marrying a dancer and having to go round the pubs with a jug like someone from the circus? If I had any spare money, I'd go and see him over there and bang his and his dancer's heads together, and show them that their affection would soon go up in smoke.

And you have to carry all that trouble like a heavy weight on your heart, while the field calls out and constantly keep you in line, body and soul. It would do someone so much good, to sit down and think quietly on all his sorrows. One would be able to empty the sorrow like a barrel, bucket by bucket. But there's no time for that. It goes on splashing about in your head. You have to provide manure, look after the animals, you must plough, sow, mow, all at the right time, not an hour must be misused or wasted. Your field must remain young and full of courage, and the frail lady from the chateau keeps banging on about her money. Ah! The field that otherwise is a pleasure is now a burden. You work in anger and your premonition tells you it's all going to get even worse.

'No, life is no laughing matter,' says the priest as he comes in, and he adds that our Fons's sweetheart, Frisine, is getting married to the sand haulier. They came to see him yesterday for the banns to be read.

'Control yourself, Root. Control yourself, man.' I had already jumped up. 'You're not obliged to keep the child. The law does not allow one to trace the father of the child and orders the mother to keep the child.'

'She can have it back tomorrow. As sure as I'm Root!'

No sooner had the priest gone than you had the tableau! Our Fien sat crying into her apron. She came and stood in front of me. She tried to hold my hand, but I dared not give it. We farmers don't do things like that. 'Root,' she sobbed, 'oh no, leave her here, if she doesn't want her, after all she's our Fons's. She and he are like two peas in a pod. Let her stay here, let it stay here. Come and stand by her cot. Look at her sleeping, poor lamb. Perhaps she's dreaming that tomorrow she can ride on your knee again to uncle Ferdinand, and God knows how badly off Frisine will be, and that sand haulier, who's always drunk, such an uncouth chap…'

'She's going! She's going,' I cried, 'and no not another word about it or I shall hit the bottle for the next three days.'

But that night I couldn't sleep, not a wink.

In my imagination I saw how I was going to get rid of the child. I would take her by the hand and say: 'Come on Liesken, we'll go and buy cakes,' and suddenly I would throw open the door of her mother's house and shove her inside. In my imagination I stood listening at the door and she would shout: 'Grandad! Grandad!' Or perhaps she wouldn't shout… But I would shout, because she wasn't sorry, and didn't love me enough. It went on all night again and again trampling over my conscience. The sweat was dripping off my body and suddenly I jumped up. I could no longer control myself and said as if to a room full of people: 'If anyone lifts a finger to take her away, I'll tear his head off!'

Then our Fien kissed me for the first time in many years.

We kept our Liesken. I went to buy cakes with her the next day. We wrote to our Fons to tell him. No reply, but a lad from the next village, who was also based in Arlon and was coming home on leave came out of his way to tell us that Fons had been given three weeks in the guardhouse. He had had a nasty fight with a new lover of his dancer. She was tired of our Fons and with the help of the new man had kicked him out.

Two months later his time was up, he told us that he would like to come back home, that he had caused us a lot of suffering, but his eyes had been opened to the good lessons of the priest, and he would be very careful in future.

'Our Dear Lord has heard my prayer!' said our Fien.

'Let's hope so,' I said, 'since God and paper are long-suffering.'

We didn't say much when we saw him again and said not a word about the past. When he saw his child he said nothing, then turned round and sobbed a little, and went to have a look at the cowshed. The next day he was behind the plough.

He was not very talkative and never said anything about over there.

Well, silly things:

'Over there I saw lightning strike so hard the trees fell off the rocks', or: 'Once when I was on sentry duty a wild boar ran out between my legs.'

It was a quiet house again, an anxious quiet.

On 1 October our Sus married his Irma and moved to near Aarschot as an asparagus grower.

In the winter as I'm sitting smoking a pipe in a group after mass, Franelle says:

'Your Fons was seen with that black-haired one.'

Usually I have my five pints after mass but now I went home like a shot.

He sat reading the Sunday paper. I put my hand on his shoulders:

'Is it true about Frisine?'

'It's none of your damned business.'

'If you do wrong it is.'

'Look at yourself!'

A slap in the face.

But oh dear me, it was our Fien who caught the blow, by jumping in between us. I half killed him, I couldn't stop showing him who was master. No so much out of rage, more because he had accidentally made me land a blow on our Fien. They went to fetch the priest. Of course I stopped hitting him then.

'Root lad, I ask you, you could kill someone like this.'

'A shame that God didn't make me an Abraham, father, he wouldn't put a ram among the thorns for this Isaac.'

In our house it was as quiet as the grave for days. A fortnight later, on a Sunday morning, our Fons says after coffee:

'I'll go to the eight o'clock mass with the little one.'

That seemed to me so strange, with that two-year-old

child, to such an early mass, in such bitter cold. As he goes away over the snow, I say to our Fien: 'Now he's playing the Christian!'

He doesn't come back for lunch. At nine o'clock at night he is still not there and that with a child of two. Our Fien makes inquiries with the neighbours. I search the pubs: I'm bound to find him somewhere drunk. No sign of Fons or a child anywhere. I go into the 'Drummer'. And the moment I come in it goes absolutely quiet. Everyone looks at me, and my heart stopped with fear: 'What is it? Do you know something about our Fons?' Their heads drop. 'Speak, for god's sake… 'Surely he hasn't drowned, has he? And the child?…'

The I saw them all smiling quietly, they were pretending, and suddenly Franelle's son jumped up.

'The water's too cold for that now, Root! He's done a bunk with his magpie, and with the child too.'

'On the four o'clock train,' said the Twister.

In a flash to Frisine's house. Her husband lay there like a worn-out clothes brush, drunk and lame in bed. Her mother, a woman who had been beaten out of her wits, said in a squeaky voice:

'If you hadn't be against it the from the start, none of this would have happened. My daughter will have a better time than with that old drunk…'

Days and nights creep past in fear and worry. Where is our Fons? Where is our Fons, what's he doing, and the child Lieske who had become our child. Won't she perish? Isn't she screaming for us?

The constable will look into it, he says every time. Look at our Fien, always thinking, with raised eyebrows, at her work and at table. She doesn't talk about it and her whole heart resounds with it. She is fading away. You raise your fist at the distant landscape, but you can't curse. It's your blood and it calls even louder when things go wrong.

I so often wish I were dead, were shovelled into the ground and knew nothing more. Because there's so much darkness in the future. You feel it coming. It's part of your life that's coming. Why do you go on living? After all, you can't ward it off. So what am I waiting for? Or is that part of my task, which I must still complete, before I fall from the tree like a pear? Life begins like an organ, that is to lure us in, but once inside they've got you and never let you go, and now you can share part of the pain that hangs over the world.

Is that Your pain, O Lord, which is so heavy that we have to help you?

The following summer I find our blind Amelieken cuddling with Franelle's son. Blind, and still the eternal fire of love. But I shoved my fist under Franelle's nose: 'See, neighbour, it doesn't matter how, but if it ever goes wrong, then your son will marry a blind wife, otherwise you and he will be for it. I'll do ten years in prison for that!'

'I kept it from our Fien, others came and told her. Through all that fear, bad expectations and grief our Fien became a person you couldn't talk to. Always thinking about our Fons and his child, and about our Amelieken. You could read the grief in her eyes.

Now they had seen our Fons in Lille, now they'd heard he was working in the coal mines.

Our Irma, a strapping daughter, nevertheless gets married to a bricklayer's mate. Two months afterwards things went wrong with Frisine's bedspread. Frisine had left that bedspread behind at ours, and must have forgotten it. While Fons is abroad with her, our Irma crochets the spread further, and now she wants to be given it. Our Fien refuses. She's right. 'That bedspread belongs to our Fons,' she said Our Fien is a fair person. Now our Irma doesn't come into the house anymore and if she meets me in the street she makes a detour, as if for the Wandering Jew.

Things like that get to you!

Our Fransoo, my brother of the friars of Dendermonde, manages to transform one of the girls, our Anna, into a nun, there under lock and key, and she has the audacity to write: 'Dear parents, now I am about to take my vows, everything will be finished between us. You will be as if dead to me and I shall belong to Our Lord alone.'

O Lord, You have given me them, You have taken them away from me. Blessed be Your name. I say that too, but against my will. I can't bear it. Lord, forgive me, but You've not made my spirit strong enough to be able to resign myself happily to this.

We can't do anything about it with our hands, but we do it with prayers, pilgrimages and novenas, and let us hope it will all contribute to our salvation!

Ha! Children, whether they die or move out of your house and your heart, they cover you with shame and sorrow, and all the reproaches you pile on their heads hurt you as if they were directed at you. O Lord, they're dearer to me than anything, and to make each child happy I'm ready to die as many times.

Our Dear Lord, I am carving You in wood. In the winter it's become almost a daily prayer, like our Fien praying the rosary by the hearth every day. Under my hands You are just a piece of wood, but gradually You are coming more and more to life. You are becoming something I love and at the same time am afraid of. With You I seek consolation for my misery, and immediately I feel my misery more acutely than at other times. Because I think more of mine than Yours. Forgive me. It might be better if I put You away quietly in the loft unfinished, and went and played cards with the neighbours. But sorrow seeks sorrow.

And I don't dare ask anything of You, O Lord. I am ashamed to ask anything of You. You who suffered and still suffer for our sins, how could I dare beg You for anything, I who am so full of sin.

No, I don't dare ask You: Rescue us from misery.

I hear You answer: and what about me then, Root?

I don't dare ask You: Bless my field.

When I see your wounds and think of your words, how could I dare ask you:

Hold Your umbrella over my field and let Oxhead's be under water. Because if his crops fail, mine will go up in price.

I would like to ask you: Pull the knives out of our Fien's heart. But You Yourself planted a knife in the heart of your Holy Mother.

My God and Lord! No, don't let me ask anything, every question is one more wound, for every question is self-interest.

No, I won't ask You anything. I have too much respect for Your pains and sorrow. But I will ask Your saints. They are something like parishioners of our home, or distant relations, more ours.

No, I ask nothing of you. I want only to worship you!

But via the two St Anthonys, with and without a pig, St Leonard, St Medard, St Gommarus and St Isidore I shall have my sad message delivered to you.

Forgive me, Our Lord, I am just a farmer and a farmer can be forgiven much, provided he worships you.

And I do from the bottom of my soul!

V

TO be a good farmer one must be able to derive pleasure from one's field. There is a lot to enjoy, if the heart is not bunged up with care. One must be able to give oneself and free and untrammelled to one's field. Then that large farmer's body greedily swallows up all its delights.

Especially if you are in prison, doing eight months for poaching, you are mightily aware for the first time of how fine and pleasant the life of a peasant farmer is. Then one gets angry with oneself for having occasionally grumbled because the work was so hard. Ha! How I regret my whining and lamenting. Just release me from these four narrow walls, and you'll see Root really spread his wings!

In the silence of the prison all those beautiful hours traverse your heart like dreams. Ai! That I have to count the days for poaching one little hare, because I wasn't sentenced for the hundred others that no one knows anything about. So, eight months' imprisonment for one little hare. The world is badly apportioned. That God created the hares and the pheasants solely for the gentlemen in their chateaux, is something I can't accept.

I did time for this in the past, two weeks. Jan Vernilst, the fellow is long dead, was poaching with me. We had to run for it. He was caught and the bastard betrayed me. I have always sworn they'll never catch me red-handed. I kept to that for years. But the last time on a foggy morning I took two hares from the nooses. I go homewards as easily as a cat down the back roads. I stand behind a haystack checking there is no danger and then I feel a big hand on my shoulder: 'Now I've got you, Root!' Was I supposed to kill him, that gamekeeper? I suddenly thought of our blind Amelieken and I said: 'Do your duty, man.'

Eight months.

Now I know how beautiful and good the fields are, that's a lesson, a punishment for my complaining.

From now on when I'm free and have to work like an ox, a donkey, a slave, I shall still sing Hallelujah and little Jesus thanks!

The field churns constantly through my mind. Our Fien and the children too of course, but especially our field.

Ha, what a youthful feeling it is at break of day, to pull on your work trousers, pop outside and feel the cool of the morning rustle over your skin. The mist is still lying on the fields. The crops, the herbs, the grass are saturated with drops of dew. It is so lovely and so quiet, close by and far into the distance. You're sorry you have to cough, the sun breaks through the fog, and the smells of the fields roll around in your head. You smell the clover, the corn, the water of the stream, the manure, the flowers, the honey, you listen to the lark. And you stand breathing in your doorway, imbibing the morning like a cool drink, and enjoying the growth of your crops, your work that lies there so lovely, orderly in in furrows and plots like beautiful carpets. You perk up with happiness and will to work, your blood trembles and you throw open the cowshed doors richer than a king. Ha, that warm smell of animals and manure.

You bid good day to the animals and you can tell from their eyes they are pleased to see you. You stroke them, speak to them and they answer with boo-eeh, meey, boo. Their tails twist and wag and show the joy in their hearts. The horse neighs, the cock crows. You light the fire for the animals' feed and for the coffee.

You milk, your forehead pushes against the cow's warm belly, you play the carillon with the udders and the milk swishes into the bucket, singing and dying away.

Ha, all is well. Every minute of the farmer's life is beneficial, and makes your blood glow. Now I see how beautiful it all is. Minute after minute I weigh it in my hand, but if you are actually in the midst of it you get angry about this and that and see nothing of it.

But I promise to enjoy it in future. It must not be that the memory is more beautiful than the reality.

And then ploughing the field with the horse. The soil that rolls open, the land that gleams and steams. Bottles of medicine open and the sun caresses your body. One furrow appears alongside the other, orderly and dead straight, and tomorrow I shall strew them with whole handfuls of seed. I shall stare at the first shoots with hope and longing, see them grow and bear fruit. You know every plant. That one is doing well, and this needs more courage.

Ha, the whole day lies ahead of you, from morning till evening. You can sow, pick, plant, put on manure, you smell of the earth, you can taste it, it is fixed in the grooves of your hands. You're proud of your work, pleased about the harvest, you're your own boss and your own king. I see it all before me, in a completely different light than usual. And then the pleasures during the work, that one can only appreciate when one can no longer experience them. Like the coffee with that good wholesome farmer's bread that our Fien can bake so tastily. Quickly roasting a dozen frog's thighs over a wood fire, a gin at the Twister's place, a pint in 'The Drummer' and being able to put your lips to a full pail of milk. But the pleasures that work on the heart: when you sit and charge along alone in your cart and see the land opening up from a high vantage point, and when you return home in the evening with one child on your back and one holding your hand.

All days are different and just as good.

When thick fog covers the land, people look inward, and I sometimes need that. Or the sun beats down, it's as if you're in an oven, but you know that that the corn is in full flower. When it rains and the crops gleam and you leak like a dog. Yes, I so like seeing the first leaves falling from the trees, when the advent of the young peas breaks open the ground. Let the snow lie a metre thick, let the well freeze up, I work in the barn, I have a chat with the blacksmith, I chop wood, I sit in the warm cowshed, I go poaching, or I carve the Christ on the Cross.

No, they won't beat us down. The farmer's trade is good and glorious. God give me back my field!

Our Fien comes to visit me every month with several children. She brings the fields with her with the smell that hangs around her, a smell of milk, fireplace and cowshed. I see the distance of the fields in the look in her eyes. I feel the air on her blushing cheeks. I smell the earth on her hands. I suddenly become aware of my animals, the ham, the red cabbage coated with dewdrops, which do not fall off, beets weighing two kilos (without chemicals), the wheelbarrow squeaks, my spade gleams, the sun slides its rays through the wood, the damp rises from the streams, the morning wind plays in the sleeves of my Sunday shirt. Ha, I feel the fields physically. And with the hand that I give to our Fien I also shake hands with our field.

And then eventually, when my time is done, with as many children as she can, she brings the cart to take me from prison. We're so happy, we first go to church in the big city to pray a rosary. Then in a market stall I buy a trumpet or something for the children, and we start eating the sandwiches that Fien had brought with her with some of our ham in them, in a quiet pub. Our Fien tells me the news. For the last two months she was unable to come because of illness. Still no news of our Fons. Frisine has left him and is living in Antwerp with the child. She does cleaning for a living.

They fished her partner, who had disappeared without trace for a long time, out of a pond near Moll. The Oxhead's wife is dead and buried, died in childbirth. The Twister is getting married and Franelle lost an eye chopping wood.

Our Fien really frightens me. For the past eight months I've dreamt so beautifully of our field that prison was almost a pleasure, and suddenly you get a whole string of accidents that have struck your neighbours poured out over you. But it won't happen to me, God will help me and my courage is like steel.

The neighbours welcome us, as we come round the corner in the cart. They have decorated their windows, even the Oxhead, and put a kind of maypole outside my door. When Jef den Dries, Franelle, Michel van de Suetekens and so many others came back from prison for poaching, I also made decorations. With us going to prison for poaching is an honour. The hares belong to us too, it's a natural law. Adam was a farmer too. A farmer's right that not even king can change.

I buy rounds in the pubs, but before I go to bed, I still have to have the pleasure of stamping on my field with a heavy tread and experiencing the generosity of the fields. I feel like a tree that sucks up the sap from the earth.

But our Fien calls and we go to bed, in fresh sheets.

It was as if as if we were only eighteen. I hadn't been home for eight months!

And the next day back to work with fresh heart. First open your lungs in the doorway like a harmonica. See the lark rise, sniff in the smells, then to the cowshed. Exactly as I had dreamed of it in prison.

But the animals no longer knew me. They had a different look, language, tails. That will right itself. In the first few days you constantly taste the goodness of a farmer's life, but soon they shoot arrows at your peace of mind. Trouble and care, illness, difficulties with the children, and paying the rent, but I will, I will, I will take my pleasure from my field and my work!

To hell, dammit, with our Fons, with our Irma, with our Fons's black cat, who is back living in the Plattekeeshoek and tortures us by no longer letting her child come and see us. To hell with the frail lady from the chateau. To hell, to hell with it, leave me alone. Let me be a farmer. A complete farmer. God made me a farmer, for God's sake let me be one! I bottle up my misery, I don't want to acknowledge it, I don't want to know about it.

But winter descends on us and I don't dare take the Christ down from the loft, not wanting to see my misery reflected in his suffering. Those who are not reflected don't see how ugly they are. I want to be happy. It's my right.

At New Year the children from the village come and sing. It's snowing thick flakes. I sit by the fire smoking a pipe, with a bowl of coffee in my hands. Children come. They are given carrots or an apple. Four girls come. There is a little tot with them. As our Fien is giving fruit to the four of them, she suddenly cries out: 'Good Lord, but it's our Liesken!'

'Grandad, grandad!' A minute later she was sitting on my knee.

'Tell Liesken's mother that we'll bring back the child this evening, it's terrible weather now.' Before evening falls, one of the children comes and says: 'Liesken's mother says that Liesken can stay here for a few days.' Oh, how happy our Fien is. She brushes the tears from her cheeks. I am even happier, but I don't show it. And our Fien never stops saying: 'We have to find our Fons, they have to marry, that drunk is dead now, and everyone will be happy.

And I said to the constable: 'Have another look for our Fons.'

It was getting on for Candlemas, and that same evening I had brought home a nice hare, although I had promised our Fien not to poach anymore, but the urge is stronger than any will, and that evening the constable comes in. He gave me a piece of paper and said: 'You must go and see the inspector of police in Antwerp tomorrow morning.'

'Is our Root going to be locked up again?' asked our Fien.

'Only if he's done something wrong, otherwise not,' said the constable, and went off.

What's it about? That hare? I couldn't sleep all night and the nights last so long. I just drank coffee. Back to prison? But they hadn't caught me, had they? And what did that inspector in Antwerp have to do with it? At four o'clock I could stand it no longer, I dressed and got going. I hear our Fien give me her blessing from behind the door.

On foot to Antwerp, three hours away. No, not in the cart. That way I could march off my disquiet. By eight o'clock I'm at the town hall. The inspector was a big chap, who was just drinking coffee from a tin mug. The policeman who had brought me in, said my name and without looking up the inspector says:

'Take him on through.'

The blood sank into my shoes. This is prison.

'What have I done, sir,' I asked.

'Nothing man, but would you recognise your son, your son Alfons?'

'Of course, dammit, I'm his father, aren't I!'

'A chap has hung himself, and they say it's your son. Suicide. We have to know, so we can write him off. Go along to the hospital, that's where he is.'

I went with the policeman.

'Come on,' he said.

Our Fons has hanged himself, that was all we needed. At the same time it was a blow and a relief. We're rid of him. Finally. Still, I wished it wasn't my son who had hanged himself.

I am brutish and anything you like, but it would break my heart if one of my children could not die a Christian. What else is marriage for but to bring up children to God's glory? But that can't be our Fons, it can't be, it can't be!

Oh, how sad our Fien will be. Better a lost sheep than a cursed soul. O Lord, don't let it be our Fons. And if it's him, don't let me recognise him! Oh poor our Fien. Fieneken, Fieneken, I thought, you've been through a lot, but this is the fatal blow, the great sabre.

We reach the hospital, a big gate, we go along corridors that smell of doctors, through a courtyard

and they take me into a small building. There three
corpses are lying on stretchers under a sheet, an old
man pulls off the sheet from the middle one.

How awful! A blue, swollen face, a lop-sided
mouth, green lips… Fons… it's our Fons. Poor Fien. I
close my eyes, I can't look at it.

'Do you recognise your son?' asked the policeman.
I stood there with my eyes closed. No, I wouldn't open
them, because on a second look I would call out his
name desperately. And now I said: 'It's not him… Our
Fons had a big mole here, (I point to my left breast),
a mole, look…'

I hear them fiddling with his things.

'This one doesn't have a mole,' they both say,

'You see that he hasn't got a mole,' I say.

'So he's not your son then.'

No, it's not him. Our Fons had a mole here.'

'So "unknown", porter.'

'One for the amphitheatre,' said the old man.

'Come on,' said the policeman

When I opened my eyes the sheet was back on top.
We went outside.

You're not used to that, are you, as a peasant, seeing corpses?' said the policeman. 'You're completely
shaken up and you such a big guy. Oh, we see that
every day, it doesn't affect us at all.'

'You're tough guys,' I said with a lump in my
throat. 'Yes, each to his own trade.'

We came back to where it smelt of doctors, and as
the gate opened, I asked:

'Is that it?'

'What else would there be to do?'

'Will you come and have a pint for your trouble?' I said.

He looked around and without replying went straight into the pub opposite. I followed.

Ha, if only I could get stinking drunk. My father's heart was so shattered with grief.

He told me about those who had drowned, those who been stabbed to death.

'And will that chap be buried with a mass?' I asked anxiously.

'Yes a short mass for the poor or simple is read out, I don't know.'

'And what did that old man say about that theatre?

'The amphitheatre? Well, that corpse will be dissected by students studying to become doctors, cut up into pieces and examined and tested with magnifying glasses. When most of the flesh has been removed he'll be boiled in a large pan. Bouillon, ha, ha, ha, and then they'll put all those bones, head and ribs back together, with iron wires, and make them into a skeleton. That will then be sold to those men studying to become doctors. You mustn't give me such a terrified look, the men have a skeleton like that standing in their bedroom, which they use as a coat hook and stick a pipe in its mouth. Those lads have fun with them.'

'So that chap won't be buried? I asked in pain.

And the policeman replied, looking outside: 'They put stones in the coffin. Cheerio, so long mate, my boss will be here any minute.'

He finished his pint and was gone.

I no longer know how long I stood there as if struck by the hand of God. But suddenly the landlady said: 'Are you sick, man?'

'Yes, yes,' I said to be rid of her, and I went out like a criminal.

I tried to find my way back to the police station, I saw it from a distance, I had to restrain myself in order not to fall on my knees and confess everything. What were they going to do with our Fons? God of the highest hilltop, I must keep this from our Fien! But if I confess, then he won't be boiled down, won't be cut up into pieces and he will have a nice mass, a nice mass, even if it costs the shirt off my back. But then our Fien won't dare leave the house again, and our Fons's name will get into the newspapers.

In our shitty village to have hanged oneself is a stain that is borne by several generations. What to do? What to do? If I'm silent no one will know a thing. Over there a policeman comes walking along. He is going to read my guilt and my doubt in my eyes. I turn round and go back. On foot. At home I'm going to explain everything to our Fien and let her choose.

I tell her everything that happened up to the viewing of the corpse.

'But it can't have been our Fons? But it can't have been our Fons?' she had kept saying.

And each time I had answered: 'Listen.'

When I said that they pulled the sheet off the corpse, she pulled at my coat and cried out with such wild words and despairing looks—'It can't have been our Fons'—that I didn't dare admit that it really was him.

The woman would certainly have dropped dead.

'No, it wasn't our Fons.'

She wept into her apron with happiness.

'And how could you see that it wasn't him, Root?'

'Well. This man had a big mole on his chest and I know for certain that our Fons didn't have one.'

'That's true,' she said, 'he didn't have a mole here.'

And then she looked at the Virgin Mary, so full of pleading and thanks that none of her children should die an un-Christian death.

'So, a wild goose chase,' I said with feigned indifference, 'and the best thing is not to say a word to anyone about it, Fien, or to speak about any moles, or else they'll say it was our Fons.'

'I understand,' she said seriously and determined to keep mum.

Naturally I didn't say a word about that boiling down, bouillon and skeleton-making.

Tomorrow I shall tell the priest everything and have masses read for our Fons. I'll save the money from my Sunday pints…

But that evening I take Our Dear Lord of the Cross down from the attic again, for my grief was too great not to need consolation.

And to give everything an appearance of happiness, while our Fien prays and the children look at the holy pictures, I sit and sing quietly so as not to sob:

> Silvery moon, silvery moon!
> In the heavens I see you shining,
> In the heavens you appear soon!

VI

'YOU mustn't complain,' said the priest on the way. (I had been to call for him to visit our Fien, who was lying in bed with cramps around her heart.) 'All the bad luck strikes the farmers, you say. That's wrong, Root. It's not because you're a farmer that you endure sorrow and misery, but because you're a human being. The same thing as happens to you can happen to a grocer in town, a pub landlord, a pharmacist or a banker. Or do you think that they don't suffer the same with wife, children, illness and business? Wherever there are people there is sorrow. Adam did that to us. Console yourself, man, that you still have the farmer's trade to be able to forget your worries and find succour. Those in town don't have that resort. They climb up the wall, they flee into the fields precisely to seek consolation. And they see you ploughing or mowing and sowing, and they sigh: "How happy the farmers are. If only I were a farmer..." Of course, Root, that breath of fresh air, that silence and that beautiful view into the distance, those smells of hay and soil, all that is good balsam for a wounded heart.

Ask the poets, the painters, the philosopher what the most beautiful business is: the farmer's trade. Root, they praise it, they paint it, they study it. Because after the priest the farmer is closest to God. We priests look after the spiritual welfare of people. You farmers their physical maintenance. Through your dogged work people enjoy the good fruits of the earth, the meat, the honey, the bread, the wine, milk and beer, and they obtain leather, wool and flax to clothe themselves. You are truly the servants of Our Dear Lord, the workers in his vineyard. One can take away everything from the world, the jewellers, the artists and professors, but if one takes the butter away the world is done for. You yourself don't know how beautiful you are, you farmers, or else you wouldn't talk like that.'

Thus spoke the priest. All nice words when you have the wind behind you. Then it is blissful to hear such things, then one walks singing behind one's plough. On a print we have at home the farmer's life is also so splendid. It's called the Angelus, a New Year's gift from the newspaper. In it a peasant farmer and his wife are in a potato field praying to the Angel of the Lord. I know nothing about painting, but I have often said to myself: 'Those two must live in a marzipan house. They have children without snotty noses, don't know any frail lady from the chateau, don't stink of sweat and their feet have never felt manure; they won't get any calluses on their hands and no bent back. They play farmers like our children play "rich madame".'

The priest talked to our Fien

'You must fetch the doctor, Root.'

'Is it so bad then, father?'

'Life is no laughing matter, friend, you fear the doctor, like a confessor, and they both serve to cure.'

I sent for the doctor: 'A weak heart,' said the clown. 'Nonsense, doctor,' I said. 'Her heart is stronger than yours and mine. If you'd been through what that woman has been through, you'd have vanished long ago. There's too much sorrow in her heart.'

Of course he prescribed an expensive medicine. And of course, it didn't help. The sorrow had to be lifted from her heart. I sent for Aloiske. He exorcised her, pulled a few ugly faces with some kitchen Latin, but that did no good either. I knew the remedy. Telling her the whole story of our Fons and taking away the fear and that anguish in which her heart was trapped. First I talk to the priest about it. 'Say nothing and sweat,' he said, 'or her heart with burst into pieces.' Ha! That was hard for me and so terrible for her. Hearing her each time between two cramps complaining to me and to the cross above the bed: 'Oh, I wish our Fons was with me now. If only I could see him again... He's still alive, I feel it. A mother's heart doesn't lie... oh Joseph and Mary, you who searched for your son for three days and finally found him among the scholars, why can't we find our Fons? I'm a mother too, aren't I?... Root, talk to the constable again and tell him to investigate...'

And you have to be silent! You have to bite back the word burning on your lips.

For two years this secret has hung between us like a fog. For me a double torture to hear it talked about and have to keep silent.

'But what if she dies without hearing anything, father?'

'She will hear in the hereafter, Root, where everything is seen with a spiritual eye.'

'Will she go to heaven, our Fien, father?'

'No, Root, she won't go there, she will be hauled up there by the angels, your wife is one of those Christian heroines who don't find their way into the almanac. She has had much grief, has wept a lot, but has accepted it with resignation. You must not think, Root, that to be a saint you have to always look northwards with one eye and at your big toe with the other. Your wife is one of those fresh figures who are holy without seeming to be. In any case you can take a leaf out of her book, Root. Where she folded her hands, you went in for devilment, swearing and drinking gin, What's best? But that's also why she is so loved by Our Dear Lord.'

'If He loves her so much, why doesn't he leave her with me, whom she loves too, and her children. If she's going to heaven anyway, why can't she wait another twenty years? On the other hand, there are even more saints in it and heaven is very beautiful. The more the merrier.'

Our Fien got worse, and the pains did not relent. At first sight one would have said it was play-acting. She lay there so blushing, round and tender. But her lips were as purple as a red cabbage. Her eyes glittered more with fear than with life. Her breath was short, and the sweat fell in drops from her cheeks.

'If only the weather would change, it might be better,' said the priest. 'She needs fresh air and this air is scorching.'

Yes, it was the most terrible summer I've known. We were approaching harvest time and it hadn't rained since the beginning of July, not a cloud appeared in the sky and the sun beat down so that the ground cracked and all the greenery shrivelled up and faded. There was a constant arid, hot east wind that played in the hearth with a soft whistle and, still whistling, skimmed the fields. The dust sometimes hung high above the trees, then it ran across the roads like columns, the ground was like pepper and hot as pepper for the crops. The crops were grey with dust, The streams and ponds had dried up. In the chateau pond the carp lay exposed and rotting. In the Nete one could find some stinking muddy water at high tide. It was like a visitation, as if the whole world had been struck by the evil hand and everyone was bound to die of heat and thirst. A steel-grey dry air, as always enough to drive you mad, the sharp whistle of that dry east wind, which charged across the land and made the trees rustle day and night. In the morning not a drop of dew, never a cloud in the distance, nor in the summit of heaven, no hope of a shower of rain to refresh the earth. The animals longed for the cool water, for the juicy grass. Sometimes one had to get up and night and try to make clear to them in words that it was not possible, but that it would soon rain and they would be able to drink as much as they liked. The farmers could then happily say to the priest that they had not christened the milk. A litre of water had almost the same value as a litre of milk. A novena was held for rain and the procession went through the fields every day. Ay, what a procession. We could not see each other for dust, it stuck to our sweat and we soon looked as black as Moors. With hymns and prayers that whole bunch of human beings asked for some simple water, which usually they carelessly spill. But it was as if the air and God's ears were also dried up. The frail lady from the chateau also joined in the procession. They may not have worried about water, there they drank wine, but for them rainwater came to represent the farmers' rent money. Oh, it was sad to see, those crops, which they had planted and sown with such industry, tended and surrounded with hope. No plants had reached their full growth and they hung and lay there pining, full of dust, tired and buffeted by the wind, shrivelled and bare, enough to make you cry. All our sweat and work, our joy and longing, down the drain. It was bad, very bad. People talked of nothing else, and as always happens, eventually we laughed about it and told jokes. The Twister said that he drank water on Sunday and in the week had watered his celery field with beer. Making a virtue of necessity. But more intense than the spectre of the fierce drought in my mind was the spectre of our Fien and her sickness. I began to shiver when I thought of her going and leaving me alone with the children.'

'If it starts to rain, carry me out into the downpour, Root, I'm burning up inside.'

I prayed for rain more for her than for the field.

And so harvest time came round. The straw of the corn was hard and tough. I was on my own with a couple of snotty-nosed kids. Where are the children now? Where's the help? Our Fien sick, our Fons dead, our Anna a nun; one lives here, the other there, our Irma, with her bricklayer and her four children, has also got her hands full. Still, she does come back home, now her mother is sick. To think that a person has to be on their deathbed before you have a child to help. No more mention is made of the bedspread. Our Sus lives in Aarschot with his large household and sends a message to say that it's very bad, but that he can't come. Our Stan, who's nine, I leave at home to look after our Fien, our Amelieken and the young kids. Our Mon, a boy of fifteen, helps me.

O Lord let not only the eye of the chateau rest on my field, but let your great eye also wander over them, and all will come right again under the glow of your all-embracing eye, and the crops will again rise full of sap and lush, fed by the cool dew of the heavens.

Shed your dew, heavens, shed your dew, says the song. Your feet drip with fat, it says in the books, but Root is content with a tear of goodness from your eyes. Choke, whistles the wind, choke says the dust, choke, rustle the trees choke one reads from the day that begins and the night that falls. Choke!

I must take on another labourer. Franelle suggests his son. Put the cat near the mouse with our Amelieken? I take Van Pul, a mature chap with a back of steel, and then I am reassured about the children and about my work. And we begin the harvest two weeks earlier than usual. We pick the corn because it's there but not with the proud pleasure and happy care of other years. It's not worth the trouble, Joseph the dreamer could not imagine scraggier ears of corn. We pick and the wind pours waves of heat as if at every step new ovens are opened. My ribs are red-hot bands. The wind blows the corn and dust in our faces, we eat sand. The salty sweat pricks the lips. A drop to drink, drink. To refresh oneself and feel fresh. Water is sacred now, too precious to pour into your body, one leaves it for the animals. We order beer, it tastes sour in the mouth; the best thing is gin. Not so much as a remedy against the heat, but mainly to be able to forget the business with our Fien, and also for the taste of course. Another bottle! And in the evening Van Pul and I are singing blind drunk in the corn. Our house is in uproar.

'Fetch Frisine,' says our Fien, 'she's a capable woman, she's not a stranger and she'll marry our Fons when he comes back.'

It gives me a shock. On top of this ghostly heat, on top of the worry about the death of our Fien, comes the enchantment of this witch. I immediately think of the business with the cart and maybe it's the heat or the gin that gets me worked up every day, I don't know, but my head is soon full of lustful visions. 'Leave her out of it, that crow's child,' I say.

'Why?' asks our Fien. 'She'll tidy everything up in here. You can't believe how much it grieves me to see everything in such a mess.'

'I'll find someone else.'

'Root, take Frisine, she knows the house and our ways.'

'I'll see.'

I never stayed long with our Fien. I can't sit by a sickbed, it makes me embarrassed and awkward, I dare not keep quiet and don't know what to say. Now Frisine is on my mind all day as I bend in the boiling sun. Am I afraid of her then? Not of five hundred of her! Am I no longer a man with a will of his own? Well, she's not coming, I'll look for someone else. And if she does come, and she dares give one sign of silliness I'll throw her out, that bad woman. My pick axe gleams. That's how the knife gleams at home in the drawer waiting for my next sin of adultery. And I try to bring that business with the bull close up as if with a telescope. I mustn't forget something like that. Well, I'm not afraid, I want to show them that I'm a man. And although I know very well that I will take Frisine on to help in the house, I will still go into 'The Drummer' and ask if they know of a girl who can help us in the house. They will have a look. Now no one can reproach me. So I go to see Frisine. She's coming tomorrow. I can't sleep all night. Doors and windows are open. I walk restlessly in the moonlight, in the garden, through the house, through the cowshed. The trees rustle in the wind, the wind whistles like a ghost round the vegetables and one hears the dust shifting. The full moon makes everything clear and mysterious. It laughs, it laughs at our effort, our en-chantment and our despair. I hate the full moon, that devilish cat's head that made our Amelieken blind. I'll quickly go and stand in the shadow of a tree to escape its influence. I feel a strange power around me, which threatens our life. How ghostly and false life is.

O Lord, great God who created everything, in all mildness and goodness, what kinds of evil things have you placed between You and us? My heart is pious and full of You, but my body that enfolds this heart is full of enemies. My heart longs for you like my animals for the pond, my body flees from you like fire. And if those two are in conflict, my will is a paper sword. Intervene, O Lord, deliver us from the evil that lies in wait for us. Let the temptation leave me, and let it rain! Let Frisine be ill!! Let it rain on the land and on my heart and I shall walk refreshed in Your ways.

My hot blood beat painfully like a hammer in my head and nothing to cool a toe, a finger or an eyelid. Not to be able to lie down coolly anywhere to be relieved from the heat from outside or inside. O Lord, let it rain! The moon laughed until break of day. And like so many days in succession the sun came like doom, without mist or dew, sharp and red over the world. I made the sign of the cross from fear and powerlessness. O Lord, let it rain!

Frisine was indifferent and did not yet pay any attention to me. She did her work well. What a fine-looking woman she is.

I had to take the cart to the Nete for water. I hurried to get home. Suddenly I pulled up. Fool! I said to myself. And I stayed waiting in the blistering sun for more than quarter of an hour by the church bell. When I got home I met the priest.

'She's gone downhill today, Root. I shall bring the sacrament to her today, while she has all her faculties. The children and the family must be warned. You must be brave, man, brave. Her life was beautiful…'

Frisine was already busy making everything in orderly and proper for the coming of Our Dear Lord.

Our Fien said: 'He must come into a Sunday house, we must receive Him properly.'

With a lump in my throat I immediately began raking and turning over everything in front of the house. In the distance the bell tolled.

While Frisine lit the candles on the threshold I quickly put on a different smock. Our Lord was approaching our house. Our Lord came into our house, He who created everything, from whose hands we eat. He does not come often to us, but when he does, he comes to fetch someone. He was coming for our Fien. Until now I had not been able to imagine clearly that she would die. But now He came, I knew down to the depth of my heart, as certainly as day follows night, so certainly that I made no attempt to ask for her recovery. And then I bent my head and said in resignation: 'Just come in, Our Lord, make yourself at home.'

Once the priest had gone, Death remained. One can feel him standing and walking about there. And then one wants silence and wants everyone to walk on tiptoe. In that silence one can hear him.

The next day the family came, mine and our Fien's. A full house. Our Fien's face was purple.

The doctor said that she must not say anything and no one must ask her anything. You can see that from here. What was the good of her saying nothing in order to live one or two more hours? Like a prayer that one rattles off, like a litany she spoke constantly about our Fons. That we must receive him well when he came back and must ensure that he soon married Frisine. Frisine cried all day. She was ugly with her red eyes. I don't know how but through the coming of our Lord, the desire for Frisine was suddenly covered as if with a lid. And I resolved today or tomorrow when our Fien closed her eyes, that I would give that Frisine a kick up the backside. I began to hate her. Was she not partly to blame for the death of our Fons? Had she not led our Fons on before and after her marriage? I'll never forgive her!

Of course the conversation turned to the drought. One person said: that it would never rain again and the world would turn into a desert. The other said that a storm would come, so fierce that the globe would split in two. We were frightening each other. At night I was alarmed by the silence.

The trees stood still, the red cabbage did not flap. The wind dropped. And the sun rose with a poisonous yellow colour. The weather changed. I was in the field digging the pepper patch when I heard our blind Amelieken call out: 'Dad, dad! Our mother!'

I left the spade stuck in the ground, I knew what it was and trotted straight home. Our Fien's lips were white. Her colour had faded to a false red. The light had gone from her eyes. The children and Frisine stood round the bed weeping. The priest came and no sooner had he seen her than he nodded to me. He meant: Root, she's going. He lit the candle.

'Is it you, Root?' said our Fien. Her right hand let go of the rosary. She sought my hand.

'Root,' she said and she smiled at the same time. 'Listen, our Fons is calling me… Why are you hiding him from me? There, there he is…' she pointed to the window… 'What does he have around his neck? Are those flowers around his neck?… Hello, Fons lad!…'

Her mouth opened and closed a couple of times, without a sound. I could no longer control myself. Even if it meant prison, I did not want to let my wife sink into the grave with a lie.

'Our Fons!' I cried, 'our Fons!…'

'Can't you see, Root, said the priest, 'that she can no longer hear. She's already with Our Dear Lord…'

Then I was able to go on bawling. I bawled till my face was wet, but in the field alone, the pleasure of letting the tears flow. And I said nothing but: 'My little Fien,' it was almost a song that I sang.

At night a few neighbours came for the wake. Normally it would have been a full house, but now with the threatening storm, for which so many nasty things were predicted, only those came who had courage and could be spared at home.

The wind came from the same direction as the rain, and when evening fell the west was full of thunder clouds. They gradually descended towards us and at eleven o'clock the first cloud moved in front of the moon. We sat praying with the door open. Lightning started to flash from all directions and the thunder did not stop. And after a violent wind, against which we had to shut the door, it started to rain, pelted with rain, and lightning flashed and thunder boomed so that the sky opened and closed. At last. But there was still too much fear of the storm to be glad. I went over and stood by our Fien's bed. In a storm she always liked to have me at home, close to her. She protected the children like a mother hen, but she felt protected by my presence. Just as if Our Dear Lord before my very eyes would cause the thunderbolts to fall on someone else. But now she was dead I went to her bed anyway, and I said: 'Calm down, Fien, it won't be so bad. Much ado about nothing.'

Ha, what a relief when the morning finally came, when the storm passed and we could open the door. Fresh, wet coolness full of smells and touching memories. As if the world began again, enough to make you kneel! Those attending the vigil went home, Frisine went for some sleep. I looked happily at our Fien.

'It's over, Fien,' I said. Life was over for her. She lay there dead. It had all been so beautiful, her willingness, her care for me and for the children and not for herself; how happily she brought the children into the world, the children who would crush her. Oh, how could I forget such a good woman for that maid with the bull? But death is like a sacred force, which makes me as big as a giant and as humble as a child. I feel myself relieved of all the tortures of the evil one. I feel strong enough to fight my way through life virtuously with my work and my children; I feel like a child ready to do what Our Dear Lord asks of a poor farmer. He doesn't ask much of us, because we have very little. It is as if everything will go better and more easily now. I am happy to take everything on my shoulders alone. Frisine can stay here, it's just an infatuation, and after all she's the mother of our Fons's child. She can stay if she wants to. She can't do me any harm anymore. A dead woman is stronger than a living one.

But now I must go to my field which is again soaked with the juice of the heavens and lies there gleaming rejuvenated and renewed. Ah, what a blessing. You can dive into it body and soul.

Our Fransoo, the friar minor, was at the funeral too, and the priest had brought a couple of bottles of wine, because I had shown such fortitude. The family on both sides was reunited and all the memories of the living and the dead were brought up. Then one feels one is growing old and that life is passing by like mist. Because of all those stories nostalgia grabs you so strongly that you would like to begin anew. Human beings are tough, they forget suffering and longing for happiness always remains most intense.

The same evening I was standing with the priest by the hedge of our garden, and while I looked at the stars, I asked him, 'And where is heaven actually, father?'

'In eternity, Root, in God's eternity, far beyond the furthest star perhaps. We mustn't let ourselves be deceived by the material world. Perhaps heaven is all around us, because where God is, Heaven is too; we learn after all: we swim in God. The question is not where he is but that he is there.'

'Yes, father,' I said, 'hard for a farmer to understand. Still I'd rather have Heaven around us, then it's
only one step. Because if I have to fly to the furthest
star, what kind of huge wings would I have to put on
to carry such a lump of farmer's flesh through space. I
think I'd never get there!'

And it really was as if our Fien was with me in that
way, as if she wasn't dead, just that I no longer heard
or felt her. And curiously, I wasn't grieving. I mean
grief in the sense that others feel grief, who lament
and take to drink.

I saw her before me still and I said:

'It means nothing, Fien, that you are dead, now
you can rest, and I'll do the work for you.'

I still saw her as she was in her youth, when I
courted her, when I married her, fresh and round. I
saw her before me, when I sowed, ploughed, milked.
Of course not real or transparent like a ghost. Just
in a vision. She walked next to me and I spoke to
her: 'Fien, tomorrow I'll select the seed for the winter
corn, on Sunday I'll pop in to see Dries about the
seed for the potatoes.' No, I wasn't grieving, but I was
alone at home. The children were playing again as
before. They were fond of Frisine and Frisine looked
after them well. I didn't like to see that. I tried to get
them to talk about their mother. Then they were quiet
for a moment and they had difficulty remembering
her; ten minutes later they were charging about again.
I was angry at Frisine because she received as much
love from them as our Fien. When the winter is over
I'll get rid of her, that Bohemian magpie. I was lonely

102

at home. As long as it was fine weather, I still had my enjoyment and exercise in the field, but now there's rain and hail and it's dark at three o'clock. Then you have to crawl from one chair to another. That laughter and screeching make your head hurt. The walls are too narrow. You look everywhere for our Fien. I wanted to hear her, see her and feel her. A vision was no longer enough, I became restless.

I should have liked to sit in a waggon and drive and drive, drive across fields and across meadows to other lands, to the moon, to the sun, on and on...

A person changes intentions and feelings seven times a day. I needed something to break and destroy in my hands. But then I had a brainwave. I took Jesus down from the loft again and got out my tools. Now I knew, I would put that Jesus on our Fien's grave.

Every evening I had him in my hands. During the work I occasionally looked up at the chimney, where our Fien used to sit and pray. Frisine was now sitting there knitting.

'If only you were our Fien,' I sometimes thought, 'how I would crush you in my arms with love.'

VII

THAT poor Jesus must be finished before spring. The spring is still far off under snow, ice and dark, on the other side of the globe; but the Jesus is still rough, clumsy and still demands lots of patience and sweat, before people take their hats off to it and say: Have Mercy on us, Lord, have mercy on us.

But he must be finished before the first spring onion peeps out of the ground.

He begins to weigh on my heart. No, it's not something for a farmer to have Our Dear Lord in his hands every day.

To see Him hanging above your bed, to feel God's eye looking constantly from the mantelpiece at your mouth and hands, that is already awkward enough for a farmer, but then sitting for whole evenings bent over him, with your knife and tools making the pain of his wounds and the grief in his heart speak from the wood, that creeps through your brain like a worm.

You no longer feel free, your thoughts keep revolving about fearful things like death, sin, hell, infinity and eternity.

Such work is good for men like our Fransoo, the friar minor. They enjoy it, it makes them happy, it's what they like, they speak and think about nothing else.

Each to his calling. Those things make me gloomy and hectic.

A farmer must be just the opposite: lucid and calm in his mind. A farm lives from the light and with the light. He helps the sun.

And if one shuts oneself up in gloom, one wants others to be the same, especially Frisine and the children. Frisine laughs and sings, whenever I've turned my back. Frisine is happy. Her happiness is challenging. When I'm there she's silent, and says and asks only what's necessary. She does her work with pleasure. Her black eyes sparkle, full of life and joy. She doesn't know why. I think that's precisely the most beautiful and most genuine happiness. Not knowing why, without reason.

I know well enough that she, the children and the neighbours call me Buffalo. It can make me furious. A buffalo! I who love my children to death, who honour the memory of our Fien hour by hour, I who love my field like a musician his organ. I a buffalo! No, it's those strange thoughts that pull me down. That's why the Jesus must be finished. I will be a good Christian soul without carving a Jesus statue. I used to be one. Oh, how often I would love to play with the children, and sing and laugh with Frisine. But when they be-come aware of me they are as quiet as mice. They used to fly and jump up on my knees. I can't start being carefree, or they would see me as mad. They think I have lots of grief and for that reason I've become so grumpy, and they want to respect this grief.

But I've already said: I don't feel grief, I've just withdrawn into my odd thoughts and strange fancies, about sin and eternity. I'm lonely and still lonelier because I no longer see our Fien before me. Perhaps that's just as well, otherwise this could have ended in a setting of that imagination in stone, and they would have put me in the asylum in Geel with my brother. Grief? Our Fien is in heaven. What more can she want? And even if I cry until I'm as thin as a mussel shell, she won't come back.

No, my condition does not issue from all that, but is caused by the work on this Christ on the Cross statue. My mind is too anxious for that. And while I withdraw more and more from the world as I carve, my heart longs and burns to be loose and free, without thoughts, to be an ordinary stupid farmer, more concerned with potatoes and manure than with the mysteries of life and death. I should talk to the priest about this, which I will never do, as he would regard me as a heretic or a simpleton.

That's why I want to be free, be able to join in conversations with people, play cards with them, be able to laugh with Frisine.

I'm jealous of her joy. I often stand behind the door listening to her singing, her playing with the children, her laughter.

106

I'm jealous, and so I start talking apparently innocently about our Fons, to tease her and make her suffer.

'Wherever can he be, our Fons?' I say.

And then she is immediately knocked off balance and starts to feel sad:

'I don't know. He upped and left... He didn't say a word for days... He cried sometimes, but I couldn't find out why. There was a worm in his heart. I said so often: "Lad, go home for a bit. Everything will come right." Then he would shrug his shoulders. I believe he's dead.'

'I think so too,' I say then, 'and I'm almost certain.'

Then she starts crying and is down in the dumps for a half a day.

I've already tried to keep away from that Jesus. I can't. It's as if he's calling, it's as if I hear him groaning in the loft.

I am hurrying to finish him. As if to be free of a burden. New Year has already passed and then you're already snuffling towards spring. Nothing noticeable yet of course, but the light leaps a few cockcrows earlier out of the night. I look forward to the good weather, because I want to be like the spring, youthful, happy and good-tempered, as if I am beginning anew, and then we'll be able to show who and what Root is! Yes, I shall go walking over fields and meadows and put out my poacher's loop.

Our Fien will certainly see it all from up there with a benevolent eye and say to herself: Good man, make the most of it.

First let's finish the Jesus.

But the most difficult thing about that Jesus has still to come. The eyes! Jesus's eyes!

Nose, ears and beard need just a last finishing touch, and I'm certain they'll be to my complete satisfaction.

But the eyes!

Will he keep his eyes open or closed? Closed eyes mean death, that says so little. With open eyes you can express all his pain and suffering. He must be able to speak to people with his eyes, as he's spoken to me for so long. Will I succeed? For example, if he happens to be cross-eyed? I mustn't make myself ridiculous for ever. What if I brought that good wood carver from the town, with the curls? To model those eyes?

He wouldn't ask a lot, because artists are as poor as farmers, I always hear the priest say. No, better no eyes unless I can put them in myself.

I went and stood in front of our mirror. To see what was best, eyes closed or open, I kept one eye shut and observed it for a long time. It was simple to chisel, a kind of mussel shell. Oh, but most Jesuses have their eyes shut. I fancied one with his eyes open.

Then in front of my mirror I pulled a sad face and tilted my head to one side. That was much nicer and, looked at closely, not so difficult. That was how you did it. Make those mussel shells into a kind of buttonhole and in that buttonhole inscribe a circle with a hole in the middle. Nothing else… So I went to work. After mass I stayed in the church till everyone had gone. Then I stood on a chair, to study the eyes of St Anthony-Abbot.

I worked patiently and thought my Jesus's eyes were good.

'What do you think of it?' I asked Frisine.

'Just like someone with a tummy ache, with his frog's eyes.' She burst out laughing and the children joined in.

'What do you know about it?' I cried in fury. 'By God you've never seen a Dear Lord… It would be better…'

I suddenly saw her eyes sparkle, angry as a tiger about to tear someone to pieces.

I meant to sling all kinds of reproaches at her. I was beside myself. After all it was her who had wrecked our household.

But her look cut my words to pieces, overwhelmed and paralysed me. And I became so ashamed of my weakness that I left with a God dammit, and slammed the door roughly behind me. I heard her swear and put a chair away angrily. 'Bedtime!' she said to the children, who dared not say another word. When I came back in later I acted as though nothing had happened. It was quiet, and neither of us said a word. Nor did we usually when we were alone. But the silence was not so noticeable. Each of us was doing our work. Now the silence pinched, a spiteful silence. And a little later, without saying anything, she went upstairs.

Something had snapped between us. As far as I was concerned she could go, the poisonous creature, as long as she left Liesken with me.

But the vixen is capable of doing me down completely, by taking the child with her.

I kept working at the statue every day, on the hands, ribs, mouth and when Frisine was not around I shaved the protruding eyes until they were closed again, mussel shells. Now I saw that the left eye had become too small, the size of a hazelnut. Sticking a piece on is not possible. So I must make the right eye just as small. But as a result there was now too little room to give him open eyes, and so I had to make them shut.

One evening Frisine was reading an episode of a novel. My rage had long since subsided but in her case there seem to be splinters persisting in her thoughts, because her words were even curter than before. And look, when I'm no longer angry, I don't want others to be angry. I wanted to make up for that angry outburst.

'Have a look, Frisine, and tell me if it's all right.'

'I don't know anything about it,' she snapped back, 'since I've never seen a Jesus.'

My blood was boiling again. That snake. I had an impulse to smash the whole Jesus to smithereens over her black head. If I were to squeeze her to death with my hands, would it not be a boon to myself and everyone? Suddenly it struck me how alone we were here, how every evening there were just the two of us here, I with Frisine, who had more than once pierced me through with sinful desires. And while my blood was still boiling with rage, I again began to want her.

What's the allure of that woman, who every time I think of her fills me with contradictory feelings, with murder and the need to embrace?

'I didn't mean it like that,' I said and made something up. I was surprised myself by my own invention, as if it did not come from me.

'Come here, Frisine, stand in front of me with your eyes closed. I can't carve those eyes out of the wood without a model.'

And she came. Now I was even more surprised. She came willingly and stood in front of me. I surveyed her in surprise, and of course the change was too great for me to make a single cut. I sat looking at her with Jesus on my knees and the knife in my hand, I saw her and the sweat welled up on my forehead. A healthy, fine-looking woman was standing in front of me, with a thick white throat, firm breasts that went up and down. Even with her eyes closed she conquered my heart. My eyes wandered admiringly over her body. What an attractive woman, a joy, a temptation, and at the same time she inspired respect and there was something commanding about her. Not a weak woman. A woman one doesn't simply grab hold of, whom one fears even and if she's not the first to fall in love, a person does not know what twists and turns he must make to win her. Ha, what a moment! I felt overwhelmed by hell and the devil.

At this moment I could equally well have plunged my knife into her breast, and pulled her to me and broken her under the weight of my passion.

Just as well that I looked at the Jesus and heard his voice. That quiet voice, which for so long had made my thoughts restless. I could have burst into sobs. Those are moments at which your soul and your body are torn apart.

'Is it finished?' she asked.

'Yes,' I said with a sigh as if waking from a drunken dream. She came and stood behind me to see whether those eyes were right now.

She bent forward, said something about the eyes, I forget what. Her hair scratched my jaw, her breath brushed my mouth.

Was this the old story of the cart beginning again?

Ha, I thought, if you hadn't been the lover of our Fons, if you didn't have this child from him… I wobbled. And I felt so clearly that I wobbled that I put my big hand over Jesus's face. He must not see this. I raised my head, the knife fell from my hands, my hand went up to her face which came closer to mine. Something blind and wild overpowered me.

At that moment the door opened. Franelle.

'Am I intruding perhaps?' he cried and closed the door. We leapt apart. With the Jesus in my arms I was at the door in a flash and dragged Franelle back inside.

'Why should you disturb us, we were just assessing him, looking at his eyes. What do you think of him, Franelle? Have a good look.'

Franelle looked Jesus over.

'Much better than before, Root,' he said. 'But don't you agree that the eyes are much too small?'

112

In order to win him over, as if to bribe him, I said in a cowardly way:

'Yes, Franelle, you're jolly well right, I'll fix that right away.'

'I just dropped by to say in passing that our Tist has had twins. I'm going to see the priest now to arrange the christening…'

When Franelle had gone I sighed, still paralysed from the shock. Now the difficulty arose of how we should regard each other. Frisine did not look at me at all. She was the same as always.

I'm off to bed,' she said. She went up the ladder with the candle-holder.

I dallied there disconcerted with my heart still beating wildly from the shock of Franelle, and now with it beating anew now Frisine was acting as if nothing had happened.

What a spider of a woman. You hang there with your faces close together hear each other's blood boil, and a second later she acts as if she's from the back of beyond.

While I'm thinking about this she comes back barefoot, jacket loose and hanging hair. She came just to get a skirt that she'd prepared. She said nothing, neither did I. She had to pass me again. My hands opened to grab her, but it was as if she smelt it, and wanted to work me up even more, and she went round the other side of the table. Halfway up the ladder she stopped.

'I've noticed you must put fresh wallpaper over the planks of my room, because there are cracks.'

Stupid that on that evening, such an evening! I wanted to go on working at the statue of Jesus. The knife was trembling in my hands, from the trembling of my heart. I continued working full of anger at those eyes with my thoughts in front of those cracks, with my cheeks still warm from her breath, my eyes still full of the image of her, half-dressed.

How are relations going to be between the two of us? Is there going to be another explosion? And when? Or is it just imagination on my part?

In any case that Jesus must now be finished quickly, otherwise it will never come to anything. I don't want to work at it with sin in my heart.

Yes, I feel it, I'm going to fall, if it goes on like this. There's nothing more to be done, at least I shan't do anything.

Little Jesus, help me! But am I shouting loud enough? Is the cry serious? Oh, my heart is burning so fiercely… By God! The eyes have gone. Pierced right through. No, there's nothing for it but to cut them out entirely.

Jesus did not want to have eyes. I can understand. He no longer wants to see me. He's right.

Now my work has gone down the drain. What do the finishing of beard and toes and fingertips matter to me, if the eyes have gone. The eyes, which have to be everything. They're nothing. They're neither open nor closed. Nothing is left, like in a burnt-out rocket.

That's the end of my work. It's the fault of my sinful heart. There's lots more to do, But I no longer dare lift a finger; the courage has gone and the industry.

Ever stroke will be a mistake, as a punishment. No, I don't dare.

The only thing left is to paint him over and try to hide my failure. I shall give him the colour of a corpse, and highlight the veins on the arm in blue. The veins that I intended to chisel thick like those on my own arms. I shall paint the drops of blood on the wounds in red, and also for those poor, ashamed eyes I shall paint blue balls, with black dots in the centre. The crown of thorns that I pondered over for so long, I shall fashion in barbed wire.

Poor, good Jesus! To think that this work must end like this! You probably did not expect this of Root, that his flesh was so weak. Neither did I, Jesus, and so I'm shocked by myself and feel not worth even a quid of tobacco. I feel ugly in my own eyes. Oh, I'm so sorry for you and myself.

In the morning Frisine found me asleep. With my face on his ribs. It turns into a fine day. The first one. With our Mon I cut the shoots off the pollard willows. And the sun shines all day and there's already a magpie in the sky. How could I be so strange and so afraid and mean-spirited yesterday? Is it the evening that brings that about? Like ghost stories that in the evening make your ears open wide and which you don't want to hear about by day. Ha, tomorrow we plough, men! And now let's forget everything again to be a complete farmer, which is the most remarkable thing of all. The splendid work in the field begins again, true with chilliness and rain, but the fine days count for two. And there are good winds that blow the evil towards the north. My blood is glad, I sing.

It is long ago since I sang.

Am I no longer thinking of our Fien? Constantly! And my heart says to her the whole time:

'Enjoy the glow of the Heavens to your heart's content. You've earned it. In any case it's better than here. And the children pray for you every day and I pray with them.'

In every woman I see, even in Frisine, I want to see our Fien.

Am I not thinking any more of Frisine? Because I'm singing?

I sing because I'm able to work in my field again, because I wholeheartedly enjoy the farmer's trade again. However, in between I still think of Frisine a lot. It's quiet between us, yet something's brewing. But look, those winter evenings, in which in the silence there was more opportunity for inflaming the heart, have gone. There is lots of work now, which means going to bed early and getting up earlier. I'm waiting for something. I myself don't know precisely what. But I'm in no hurry, as I'm frightened of it. Curious, I have it with every woman, that fear. Being attracted, yet feeling shy, like a mouse with a mousetrap. What a difference with our Fien, whom I immediately took possession of, but that was love. Now it's passion, the call of the flesh. That's also the work of the spring, both in plants, animals and human beings. I know that from the past. It makes me restless. I cannot keep to the same work. I seek and find pretexts to go home, to see Frisine, talk to Franelle's daughter or drink a few pints with Mie from 'The Drummer'. Yes, I sing with

Frisine, but the false witch acts as if there was never any attraction between us. I laugh with Franelle's daughter, I think to make Frisine jealous, and I go to 'The Drummer', more for Mie than for the beer.

That Mie was rather like our Fien and about the same age. She's a cheerful soul who can suddenly take a crazy turn.

On one of those day she brings me a pint, her husband is outside looking at a horse. And as she puts the pint down, I think to myself: I want to overcome my fear, and I pinch her arm.

'Tender flesh!' I say.

'Do that at home, Root, you've got tender flesh enough there,' she says in annoyance.

It came like a smack in the face, I felt trapped. I didn't ask for an explanation and started talking about the weather, and how we were going to have a late Easter. It weighed on my heart for the whole day.

'Do that at home, Root, you've got tender flesh enough there.' It went constantly through my head, like a ticking clock.

It's Franelle who did that to me, by seeing us bent over the Jesus together that evening. Or else it's because she can see it in my eyes. Or pure guesswork.

'Do that at home, Root.' I can't keep it to myself. I must tell Frisine. And it seemed to me a good pretext to find out how she saw me.

In the evening, when she comes out to draw a pail of water, and I am washing the winter carrots by the light of the lantern, I had to go to the market that night, I have to get it off my chest.

'Do you know what they're saying, Frisine?'

'They say so much, that I know.'

'That I'm courting you.'

She drops her pail into the well, she is so shocked.

'Who says that?'

'Mie from "The Drummer".'

'And what did you say in return?'

'I made a joke of it...'

'If she says that to me I'll chop that wicked woman's nose in two.' That was a cold bath to me. I must have expected her to say: And if we're courting, whose business is it? Then I could have put in a word. But it seemed that the news had offended her more than pleased her. Her attitude offended me, greatly. Now I wanted to win her, at any price, more to humiliate her, in revenge.

I was constantly considering how I could win her over. Her image, her presence filled my thoughts and my senses. I saw nothing but Frisine, I was as if blind to the rest of life. I tried to be with her as much as possible and to find the right moment. It was difficult. She was as cold as bluestone, there was great indifference in her eyes, which excited me even more.

'Tell me,' she said again one evening, 'you could block up the cracks in the wall of my room!'

Idiot, I thought to myself. Fancy forgetting that, not to fill up the cracks, but to peep through them!

And next morning at the break of day, I crept barefoot upstairs and peeped through the cracks. Only for a few seconds, for fear of being caught, and all day long she is on my mind, with those bare arms, that bare neck. If I can manage and dare to, I shall take that opportunity, and shall live on that little second all day long. Not with pleasure, because I sometimes hit my forehead with my fist: Root, what are you doing? Are you mad? You're old enough to be her father, I reproach myself, I dare not think about our Fien anymore. I feel a coward and ugly. Yes, what I'm doing is ugly. I avoid the priest. The statue of Christ stands upside down in a corner.

I'm scared in the evenings. I think I'm bewitched. I promise each evening that I will stop and not go on peeping. But it's stronger than I am. Will I go mad like my brother? Or may it perhaps pass once the work gets up to full speed? I'm obsessed with her. I sometimes pray, if one wants to call it praying, against the longing for you, for something from God: 'Lord, take her image from my thoughts.' Useless of course. If I suddenly threw her out and took a manly decision? Nothing so simple. I feel capable of that. But what about Liesken? The child I am so bloody fond of?

All things considered, I feel that I shall fall. I believe, however, that it won't be before Easter, because then I shall have to confess again, and I'll have the same business again as with that previous girl.

Oh, I feel as weak as a child, unhappy. I sometimes bang on the handle of my plough with tears in my eyes and try to calm myself with curses.

Does the priest suspect something? Have they been telling tales behind my back? He acts so strangely when he sees me and when he says something, his words are little digs.

The March squalls treat the land to hailstones and harsh wind. I stand silently with Frisine unloading a cart of cow dung onto the field.

The priest comes breezing past.

'We're getting a lot of peppernuts, Root!' he cries. 'Fortunately those are the last whims of Mr Winter. It's like an old fool with people!'

And he breezes on, down a side road.

The old fool? Does he know something? After all, it's all happening in my own heart. It seems to me that everyone can read my heart in my eyes. At the slightest word or attitude, I imagine I see mockery and double meaning.

'What do you think he means by that, Frisine, old fool?'

I'm sorry I asked and I go red.

'You will know better than anyone,' she says without looking round.

This the moment to say: Yes, I'm a fool about you, and say everything in one gush.

But that strong Root is just a wax doll in the presence of Frisine, and I am so silent it makes me sweat. I can't find the words. She will laugh at me, and then there can be accidents.

The next day, in the morning, on a Sunday, I tiptoe upstairs again and want to peep through the crack, when suddenly I nearly drop dead with shock; the door of her room is open. Caught! And without moving a muscle on her face, she says:

'Fasten my jacket from behind, I can't do it.'

She had a new jacket on, which was undone at the top, leaving her white round neck free. I fiddle with her hooks and eyes.

'You're trembling? What is it?'

I couldn't get one word out.

The she looked me straight in the eye, enticing and laughing.

'Do you know who the old fool is? Or do you think I don't know you come every day to peep at me through the cracks. Ah! What a wet lot you men are. I spell it out to you, you useless man. Ha! Ha!'

And what do you want? A man's not made of stone, says the song. The next day I stuck new paper over the cracks.

Even before Easter, she said it was wrong.

'Marry, Root,' said the priest, 'there's nothing so simple. There's nothing stopping you.'

'But the death of our Fons?'

The priest himself came to tell her about it.

That was a storm, grief and anger.

'Why didn't you tell me earlier? If I wasn't going to marry, I would have left with our Liesken,' and so on.

I said nothing. A priest is better with words than a farmer.

He pointed at me, as if to say: that's just the initial rage, that will burn itself out.

We were married after Lent. And we slept under the bedspread there had been so much fuss about. Now it was ours. And the next day I took the hidden knife out of the drawer and cut sandwiches with it.

I feel that I have the approval of our Fien from Heaven. My heart is content.

And back to work. Starting all over again. The land is ready. There is grist in the mill and if the wind is favourable we'll root again.

God, here I am, Your servant.

VIII

A young wife is like a rein.
One is attached to it, she pulls you and lures you the whole time with her youth and her love.

Frisine's heart is still free and full of playfulness. Grief and care have not yet formed a tough crust over her heart.

If the husband of a woman like that is also young that intoxication continues blindly. But if like me you're of mature years, and you have the first part of the mountain behind you, then love is no longer peace or release, but restlessness and hecticness.

There is a contradiction. Youth, which you thought was already behind you, rises up powerfully and with stimulation, in a body that is too mature. Your blood dances and foams, in those years when it should flow calmly through your veins.

But you don't ponder on all that, as long as the enchantment of love surrounds you. And that enchantment floods through you, makes you happy and intensely alive, fulfils you more than your work, makes you greedy, mistrustful and suspicious.

You spoon out such a love like a boiled egg.

Ha! That suspicion can pinch! What a pain!

You constantly think: Frisine is taking me for a fool.

How can such a young thing love such a lumbering old farmer! You'd like to be proud, and you don't dare.

What is it about me that she loves me so? Nothing. I sometimes stand in front of the mirror. I don't believe in her love.

You peer and spy to see if she's not occasionally friendly with the young lads. You think of Sus and Pol and your fists are ready to bash heads in.

And precisely because you can't find the slightest evidence in her of affection for someone else, you think she's a false cat, who play-acts very well.

Ha! How a jealous man is to be pitied. He's like someone who is eternally dying of thirst.

But I say you forget all those tribulations in the fire of her eyes and the warmth of her arms.

Our Fien never embraced me so passionately.

Our Fien was more serious, liked to be seen, and that produced contentment. One could be sure of her and that gave one peace to work in the field.

I remember, we went together to see the crops in the field. I was always ten steps ahead of Fien, we spoke less than five words in an hour, and yet we were so close, here in the heart.

When I walk with Frisine on Sundays, she hangs onto me, and leads me on, and yet there is a kind of window between our two hearts. I don't understand a thing about it.

At home, for example, I and our Fien could sit together for hours with having to say a word. The silence was no problem. It gave calm.

But with Frisine I can't stand any silence. If I don't take her in my arms, I don't know what to say; neither does she. The we sit on either side searching for words, but it doesn't flow, no conversation flows. Then I go off, but come back in again by the back way. There's something wrong between us.

For example, we never talk about our Fons, and every seldom about our Fien.

And I know that she thinks of him and she knows that our Fien is still clearly in my thoughts. Proof: she wears a brooch that you can open with a portrait of our Fons as a soldier in it. And she will often ask the children to do something or other:

'How did your mother do that?' Never a word to me.

Still, she's a good wife to me. Good to me and caring with the children. She's cleaner than our Fien (but our Fien had that eternal headache). Frisine takes more trouble over the washing and the household. She paints the doors herself, and whitewashes the walls like a real whitewasher. With her the chickens are not allowed to run about the house. The floor is fresh, the brass gleams and flycatchers hang everywhere.

Talking of flies. With her it would never happen, as it used to happen with our Fien. It was a real fly year then. The whole house buzzed with them, and the table was black with them. One Friday our Fien was kneading dough for white bread (white bread rarely came on the table, but she was expecting her sister), when the priest comes in and says:

'There's plenty of everything here! Currant bread. You can bake a loaf for me too!'

'Currants?' Says our Fien. 'They're flies, father. No way of keeping them out.'

He no longer insisted on baking a loaf with us.

The priest is very taken with Frisine. When he visits us he always says:

'You made a good bargain, Root.' He also tries to bring back the married children home again, because since I married Frisine they haven't set foot in the place. I don't get angry about it but when I'm on my deathbed and they dare cross my threshold, I'll throw all the apothecaries' bottles at their heads.

So Frisine keeps the household in exemplary order, and likes sewing and darning so that the children no longer runabout with a shirt tail sticking through their trousers.

But a farmer isn't too fussy about all that. He needs a farmer's wife, who lives with him in the field. Who thinks with him of the field, in spite of setbacks with children and other things. The field is everything. The rest is secondary. So you mustn't make speeches about it, mustn't mumble litanies about leeks and celery. I and out Fien understood with a single word what had to be done or not done for the field. With Frisine every time it's a whole palaver. If I said aloud to myself: 'The wind will drop tonight,' then Our Fien would prepare the carrot seed for us to sow the next day.

One word, one gesture, and everyone knew their job.

That's what you call farmers!

Frisine doesn't understand a thing about it, and with all her care and supervision we remain just as poor. But respectably. That pinched nose from the chateau can't stand that.

'Root is doing well,' she says, 'just see how clean it is there!' Does she want to put up our rent?

Frisien bore me two children, and now she's carrying a third, because I don't let the grass grow under my feet!

And I could be happy, if that suspicion didn't continue to disturb me. I walk around with jealous feelings in my heart. I'm obsessed, it's unreasonable, I know, there's no reason. That's why it's so desperate! I sometimes lie in wait, in the house or outside, I follow her. I never find anything suspicious. She doesn't look for opportunities to take a particular path or run an errand, the children look like me, like two peas in a pod, there's no sign of deceit in her behaviour and yet, and yet my heart is ground to bits by suspicion. I can no longer go poaching with peace of mind. I scarcely poach any more.

One evening when the pain of jealousy was torturing me I went to the priest, to tell him everything so that he might cure me from my despair.

It happened like this: the Twister and Franelle came to see me the previous evening. Of course, some bad stories were told about people who were not present, about Siemkens' wife, who seemed to be having an affair with the Turnip. They had been seen in the evening by the pond.

'How stupid,' said Frisine, 'to rendez-vous when there's a moon.'

That was like a hammer blow on my head. While the others went on telling stories, I was completely discombobulated. Ha! I thought, she knows the tricks! Don't meet by moonlight! Moonlight!

I couldn't digest it or swallow it. Who thinks of that if they've not had practice?

I couldn't sleep. The next day it troubled my mind. And by evening, I could have committed an outrage, if the fire wasn't put out. And in the evening I ring the priest's bell.

'Could I speak to the priest for a moment?' I asked the maid. He himself shot out of his room:

'Yes, of course, Root man, come in.

'What news, Root? Take a seat, man, and have a cigar. It's a long time since we had a chat. How are things with your wife and children?'

'Bah, well, good!'

'And Frisine? The third baby is on the way, I've heard. Halla, we'll drink to that, Root. A glass of sweet white wine from the land of the men with the curved sabres, the Turks.' He went to the cellar himself and we drank.

'Well,' he said. You've got a model wife in that Frisine, a good person. It's Fien who prays for her on high. She's much younger than you, but she's serious. I can't allow a bad word to be said about her!'

'Do they say bad things about her, father?' I said hurriedly, thankful to have heard something.

'Bad things? Say bad things about Frisine? No one! If anyone ever says bad thing about her, I'll squeeze his nose between his two ears. No one would dream of it. It's nothing but praise, compliments! Everyone says you're lucky. A good mother, and especially a good stepmother. Because being a stepmother is the hardest job in the world. A good housekeeper, and serious! To tell the truth, Root, I had definitely never expected that of her. You see, we must never throw stones at others. The good seed is in everyone, and it is just a question of surrounding it with good earth and good conditions, and it will blossom in full flower.

'You have luck with women, Root!

'First Fien, who was truly goodness personified and now someone like Frisine, who continues Fien's task so well and courageously. Well, you should occasionally say: Little Jesus, I thank you! And don't ever come to me to complain or say something bad about Frisine, because then I shall tell you it's your fault, and I'll show you the door!... Let's drink to that, santé! And now tell me what it is you want so late in the evening. I'm listening...'

The sweat was pouring off my face. Yes, what was I supposed to make up after such words, which stifled every complaint in advance. What story was I to make up in order not to look ridiculous. 'Well,' I thought to myself, 'I'll say in passing that the Christ on the Cross is finished and would he like to come and see it.'

Good God, that Christ on the Cross had stood forgotten for eighteen months in the loft. Why did my mouth suddenly start talking about that Christ on the Cross, without my being aware of it?

'Ha! That's good of you, Root. I'll drop in to see it one day soon, perhaps tomorrow even!'

'Tomorrow I'll be working in the field, father...'

'That doesn't matter. I don't need your eyes, Root, I'm all the more curious...'

'I still have to retouch it a bit, the blood on the wounds...'

'I can use my imagination, Root. And then one day we'll put it on Fien's grave! Have another drink, Root...'

A weight fell from my heart once I was outside.

I went to complain and had immediately burdened my heart with a new worry, about that Christ on the Cross; and the other worry, about suspicion, was not even eased.

What does a priest know about a wife! And what does it mean if no one speaks ill of Frisine, while my heart is meanwhile being poisoned?

This silence and the absence of comment add to my despair!

The next morning Frisine was not a little alarmed when I fetched the Dear Lord down from upstairs and sent our Mon off to the village to get paint.

'Is that in such a big hurry suddenly? The priest may pop in one of these days. He asked about it, and if it's not finished, then he'll moan again.'

It took a whole morning to get him painted. By the time the potatoes were ready he was finished. And now the hope was that the priest would stay away for a few more days, until the paint had dried and the words about it had been forgotten.

Ha! Root mustn't put a foot wrong or they'll give him a couple of blows that'll lie on his stomach for a week!

No sooner do I come home from the field than I get a ticking off from Frisine:

'What kinds of tricks are those! Last night you went to ask the priest to come and see the statue, and you say to me that he asked to himself!'

I stood there blinking. I find it hard to lie, I'm not clever at it.

'Didn't I tell you this morning that I'd been to see him?'

'You said nothing to me,' she said. 'You know that well enough. There's something wrong here. The priest said it too. "See, that's strange," he says. "He calls me to see it... Root... Curious, curious." The priest didn't say anymore, he's too wise for that, but the man didn't seem in a good mood, he felt that there was something wrong, and there is something wrong...'

'What could be wrong, Frisine?'

You can feel how weak and flat those words came out.

'What's wrong?' she cried. 'That I don't count in your eyes, that you're concerned with your dead wife the whole time, that I'm nothing but a maid here...'

Lots of tears and sobbing besides. Jealous of a dead woman!

A lot of sweet words were necessary to help things settle down. Frisine can easily cope with a harsh word, I easily lash out, but if you offended her soul, if she thought that she as a woman in love was being spurned, the old Bohemian wildness flared up. Then she took no responsibility for accidents, and it was better to eat with her than fight with her. She was full of fireworks. That gradually calmed down after all and was forgotten.

The priest acted as if he knew the answer. He kept it up his sleeve and one fine summer's day, when he saw his chance, he talked to me about it. He came for a drink of milk again.

The work was proceeding in the field and in the cowshed. I was being rather forced by the whole business to back down, but whether it was because of the harvest or the priest's words, that evening I felt much calmer, and again took pleasure in my field.

And it would have been a good year for all of us if the evil hand had not intervened. It sowed terror from farm to farm, and disaster was in the air.

The evil hand, which had taken our Polleken from us, had caused our Amelieken to be born blind, and had done so much harm to our crops and animals.

It started at the beginning of September, when the last straw from the field had been gathered in.

The constable had seen the nun with her cat standing at the crossroads at night. Two men from the Boshoek had heard mouth music flowing from one tree to another when they were coming home that Sunday evening. The cowshed light floated over the fields. Mie Verhelst could hear snakes hissing in the air when it began. The black dog had been seen and the two-legged horse, and at the pond where, so it seems, a monastery was once submerged people heard a bell tolling at dusk.

Bad omens.

And it wasn't long before one heard on all sides of bewitched cowsheds, enchanted livestock, sickness and mysterious adversity.

Aloiske, the exorcist, the Lop-sided Turf, also an exorcist, but from a different part, and the animal doctor in the village had their hands full and earned a pretty penny.

The animal doctor, who always wanted to play the crafty one, now confessed himself, when he saw the Twister's livestock dying and ailing day by day:

'After a while a person might believe the devil had a hand in it.' Franelle couldn't get any butter from his milk, couldn't make soap, and you could see his two pigs losing weight from minute to minute. The whole of the Oxhead's farm was full of slugs, the fat kind, yellow with black patches, and even at the priest's house there was an uncatchable beast in the garden, a kind of mole, but larger and with a white moustache, which in a trice ate the roots of his trees.

Everywhere people had something to complain about, one thing and another, the rats, the flies, the mould in the bread, the maggots in the turnip, and so on, and so on.

Fortunately I had been spared the evil hand up to now, but I had taken my precautions.

Bel Salamander, who for years had sat dying in her chair by the fire, had given me a powerful holy relic, which I had hidden under my threshold in the cowshed and under the roof.

The other farmers looked askance at me because I was spared the witchcraft. They almost started saying that I had a hand in it.

But one night, when I got up to visit the dung heap behind the hedge where my farm abuts the Oxhead's I hear something whispering, and a black animal jumps out from under my feet. The nun with her black cat? I go to the barn and get a threshing flail.

Nun or no nun, I'll knock the block off anyone who doesn't stay five paces away from me. I hear nothing more. But the next day my farm was full of slugs and in the Oxhead's there were none left. I quickly put my jacket on and go to Aloiske. When it's dark he comes. He goes into the garden for a while, and the next day the slugs were back with the Oxhead. Two days later they were back with me. I return to Alois. While we had to stay inside, he carried out his exorcism in the dark. Suddenly I hear shouting.

'Help! Help!' I go outside with the potato masher. There the two exorcists, Cross-Eyed Turf and Aloiske, were hanging over the hedge, outdoing each other, tugging at their collars and hair, and hitting each other in the face.

The Oxhead also came running up. I heard him say something: 'I'll... that Aloiske...' whereupon I said: 'You keep your hands off Aloiske, like I will from Cross-Eye Turf. You should have kept your slugs!'

'If they were at mine first, I expect you put them there. It's not for nothing that you've been free of the evil hand, your black crow (a dig at Frisine) has more to do with it than we know.'

If he had said: your wife is deceiving you with another man, I would simply have taken him by the arm and listened to him, hand in hand, and full of gratitude, or if he had said: You're a magician, I should have laughed, but to make out Frisine, such a good woman, to be a witch! And with that he got the potato masher in his teeth, and we were also hanging over the hedge fighting.

Franelle joined in, Frisine, other neighbours. They ran to fetch the constable, they ran to get the priest. They had to drag us and the exorcists apart, so that blood and clothes stuck to each other. I did not tell Frisine what the Oxhead had said, and he himself will have thought first of his lost teeth before opening his mouth. The conclusion was that we both had slugs. Oh dear, the little creatures could no longer choose.

On Sunday the priest gave a severe sermon about superstition. He didn't pull his punches, the priest. He was angry that we believed in those fables of the nun and the cat, cowshed light and two-legged horse.

'Fables!' he cried, 'the invention of foolish or drunken people. Who are then exploited by frauds, who swindle you out of your hard-earned money. It's a great sin to believe those things, and an even greater one to suspect each other of them. But God will punish you of little faith, for paying more attention to nonsense than to His word.

'Ah well,' he cried, 'I challenge the nun, the cow-shed light, the black dog! I challenge them! And this very night I shall stand alone at the crossroads, on the dot of twelve I shall be there, and people will see if anything happens to me!'

Naturally the whole village was standing there. Each one with a lantern. And then he gave a fine sermon:

'Either the nun exists or she does not. If she does not, not one word need be wasted on her. But if she exists, where is she then?

'I challenge her! Where is she? She's frightened of us! Frightened! It is a sign that we, as Christians, armed with the cross, are stronger than she is. And something that is frightened of us must not and cannot frighten us.

'If you stand firm in your faith, if you are virtuous then you will chase away through your attitude alone all devils and all witches. For the evil one is frightened of nothing more than the clarity of a pure soul.

'All of you go home in peace, let the cross in your soul shine and all dark powers vanish into thin air like smoke.'

Thus spoke the priest around midnight at the crossroads. He blessed us all, he blessed the fields and indeed we went home in any case with a lighter heart.

For a few days there was no more talk of magic and witchcraft and everyone was relieved. Frankly, everyone, like me, probably thought: The priest has exorcised that power, it existed and he helped dismiss it. Those men act as if that's not true. Bah, in any case we can be rid of it.

But you can't be complacent, because then people become careless and mischievous and do stupid things. It's always good and wise to keep a little fear in reserve as a brake.

It's by misbehaving that I experienced the worst misery. I'd gone to a sale, two hours away. Because of a death and the decision to abandon single ownership, a large farm was being sold together with livestock and contents. There were bargains to be had.

Frisine had said as I left: 'Home before dark, hey, you never know!' I had answered laughing: 'That won't be before midnight. I want to make the acquaintance of the nun.'

At the sale everything was far too expensive. Still there was a good whetstone which no one bid for. (How everything conspired to bring me to disaster!) I bought it. Mine was an old wreck, and this one was too cheap to leave. I dragged that heavy thing home on my shoulders down side roads.

Walking along alone, my heart again filled with jealous thoughts of Frisine. During my absence she could receive anyone. Oh! But she wouldn't do it now, she was too cunning for that. During the day never. The remark she had made a while ago: 'Stupid, those two meeting by moonlight' stuck in my mind like a pike hook.

When I drive to town on a summer night, she'll take advantage of the opportunity. Wait, I'll catch her out, and as I went along I devised a plan: The first time that I have to go to town again, I'll pretend to drive off, leave the cart and horse beyond the village, and charge in unexpectedly! I should have done that long ago! Idiot that I am!

'Something is happening with her that's not above board, otherwise my heart wouldn't be so tortured. Where there's smoke there's fire.'

I go into a pub somewhere and drink two pints, no more, I swear that on the heads of my children. Two pints, although they still maintain that I got blind drunk. The landlady complained that her man was lying in bed. He had seen the cowshed light yesterday evening, and had taken fright, so that his whole body was trembling. Yesterday towards evening he had gone to fetch wood over by the alders. The light came from a pollard willow floated over the brook and floated around his cart. He hit out at it with his whip. It stuck to his whip. Then he took fright, left the cart and horse behind and came in white as death.

'It's quite something at present with all that witchcraft,' said a farmer, who was sitting there too. 'The day before yesterday a tall, thin woman came into our yard selling matches. I said: "If you're not out of here in two ticks, I'll put a splinter in your neck." I turn round to tell our people not to buy any matches. I want to point to that woman and there's not a trace of her anywhere around, as if she'd been swallowed up by the air.'

I told them myself that a woman like that had bewitched our Polleken, and I told them about the witchcraft in our neck of the woods, and about what our priest had said and done at the crossroads.

138

And so, as we talked, it had got dark. I pay, pick up my whetstone and when I'm a good hundred metres further on, as I'm about to cross the cobbled road, my heart is seized by doubt. Along the edge of the wood is the shortest way, saving half an hour. By the highway it takes an hour and a half. Should I choose the shortest or the longest route? I'll go the longest way.

'That's pure fear!' I say to myself. I, a poacher, who was used to living in the mysterious surroundings of the woods at night and in bad weather, was suddenly frightened to follow the fringe of a wood, not to go through it, but just skirt the edge.

That's impossible! I'll walk along the edge of the wood.

I make good headway with my heavy load on my shoulder. It was dark as hell. You could see no difference between earth and sky, but from the smell of dry leaves, the smell of oak trees and from the coolness I feel that I'm following the edge of the wood. A poacher has more or less the perception of an animal. After a good half hour I have a rest, in order to shift the whetstone to my other shoulder. I look at the darkness, I listen to the silence. Not a breath of wind, and I think: At such an hour Frisine may be going out courting with another man.

Suddenly, deep in the wood, I hear a woman's laugh. I break out in a cold sweat. The nun?

'Who's that laughing?' I ask, my voice muffled with dread, and then I hear a step and a cracking branch behind me. I try to make out something. Nothing. It must have been in my mind.

'Is anybody there?' I ask with a lump in my throat. No answer. I go on, as fast as I can. I should have been through the wood long ago. The wood is less than a quarter of an hour's walk. I don't want to get worried. The priest said: 'The evil one is most frightened of a pure soul,' and my conscience is free of mortal sin. So why should I be frightened? If only I didn't have this heavy burden with me. I can go scarcely any further. Without that whetstone I'd have been home long ago. Another branch cracked behind me. And now fear seized my heart so powerfully and irrationally that I began to walk as fast as my legs and the bad road would carry me. I, Root, so feared by everyone, was more frightened than a child. Frightened of something I couldn't see. If it had been men, seven at least, I'd have smashed them to smithereens. But what can you do about something you can't see? There was something there. You can't believe what pain and distress this causes. I still kept to the edge of the wood, as if there were no end to it. I just walked, I said hasty prayers, mumbled that I had a pure soul. Enough to make you mad! Something shot away beneath my feet. I dropped the whetstone, turned left, into the wilds, left the wood behind me. And now I walked as if with wings on my heels, straight ahead, straight ahead. Why was it that I did not come across an enclosure, a house or trees anywhere? Was I on the heath? No, the earth was too heavy for that. And again I had the same feeling as just now: that for all my walking I wasn't progressing a step further. In the distance a church bell struck.

One… two… three… four. Four in the morning. I sighed with relief. The hour of the ghosts has passed. But that wasn't the bell of our village. Ours resounds more. I'll follow that bell sound, in that direction. Where was I? I was lost. Bah, then I'll wait till it becomes light.

The great panic was over, I felt thoroughly ashamed, and with resentment and dissatisfaction I set out again, hoping for the best. Tired and sweaty, I bump into a haystack. I'll wait for morning here. I could have wept for shame. Root the poacher had run away, and from what? From nothing: I could have hit myself in the face with rage, like a friar scourges himself for his sins. I decided not to after all. I would like to sleep and look for a good corner. When I get round the other side of the haystack, I see a light burning in the distance. I make straight for it. What's that? It's my own house! So was I enchanted after all? The door's not closed. The bed's empty, somebody has slept in it. Where's Frisine?

'Frisine!' I shout through the house. The children are asleep. I try to wake up our Mon.

No, I think, suddenly full of suspicion. There's something wrong about Frisine. I've finally got her! She took advantage of my absence. And there's no moonlight! Ha! She'll regret that forever! I first turn the light off, light my pipe and sit by the window on watch with a thick piece of wood in my hand. When she comes in I'll strike her down like a dog. If the Oxhead knows she's been out, he'll say everywhere that she's the nun. But I know better.

The ticking of the clock is such a nuisance that I stop it, but now it was too quiet for me, and I set it going again. My blood was pounding. It was one curse after another. The day rose into the air. I hear steps and voices. A group of people come into the yard. They are carrying something, a big package... The constable, Franelle and the Oxhead carry Frisine in, her skirts are dripping with water.

'Hey, Root,' said the constable, 'you're a bloody clever sod to do something like this to your wife. You should be ashamed of yourself! We've been looking for you all night, we and Frisine. Each in his own direction. I over there, he further over. Frisine accidentally fell in the pond. We just hope it's not too late! She was in there for more than an hour. We heard her calling, but couldn't find her. I'll quickly go and inform the doctor and the priest. Those that helped her into bed left me alone with her. I couldn't say a word.

Could I now say something about the witchcraft, I, a poacher? All I said was:

'I got lost, got lost.'

Frisine paid no attention to my words, as if she didn't believe a word. I didn't dare insist. She lay there with her teeth chattering, pale as the holy earth and groaned, with a trembling, dull voice:

'It hurts so badly everywhere—the baby will be dead, so will I... Oh, to think you stayed away so long...'

'Got lost, lost,' I kept saying. And she said:

'I thought perhaps he's in the pond... drowned going to the bell to listen. Root, this'll be the death of me. It hurts so badly everywhere. And I love you so, as much as I loved Fons... The children, oh dear.'

The doctor gave her something to make her sleep, and was going to come back in the evening. He spoke with the priest.

The priest came quickly.

'Do you have candles in the house for all emergencies, Root?...'

In the evening she glowed and looked as red as an oven.

She lay there roasting for four days, without saying a word. Now and then she gave a groan, and smiled at me or one of the children.

On the fourth day the doctor said:

'Have the priest come.'

And he came.

In the darkness I saw the lantern and heard the bell approaching across the fields.

Our Dear Lord was coming, who drives away all ghosts. No one was afraid of this light and that bell. People came and knelt in their doorways. Where he enters, He usually takes someone with him.

I knew about it from before, and still I opened the door wide, lit a light in His honour, and so that He would be able to find the way.

He had not long gone when she followed Him.

It's only later that one realises what one's lost. It's then that you'd like to drum on your face with your coconuts of hands, for your stupidity, for your lack of understanding. I held happiness in my hand and didn't appreciate it. 'Yes,' says the priest, 'life is no laughing matter. But it's mainly through our own fault that it's watered with tears. From what you tell me, I understand why that evening you sat and lied to me. Poor Root. Our Dear Lord constantly gives us gifts and presents, but we are too poor in virtues to be able to carry them. God gave you the love of a good woman, but your own faults made it a burden and a torture…'

I reproach myself with many things. It is as if I killed her.

She lies next to our Fien. They always liked each other. The earth consumes them, the heart consumes the grief, and the remnant that finally remains is a beautiful memory. A man finally rises from the past and, through the urge to be happy, looks to the future again, as if to the morning. That morning is my field!

The priest says he will look for another wife for me. Don't let him find one, O Lord! I've had two good ones, the third could be a failure. O Lord, be the mother of my children, I shall plough the field for you. Bless my hands, bless my eyes, bless my heart. And give me that solid contentment and broad resignation with which a farmer can and must work.

Add on time some sun and rain. And then I shall take the bread for the hosts and the bread for people's sandwiches happily and proudly out of the ground!

IX

FIVE years after the death of Frisine, the priest finally found me a new wife.

The third!

I almost went to pieces when he arrived with the news.

'You must marry, Root, all good things come in threes. It's hopeless as a man alone to care for the household, the children and the field. It's been long enough. You're going to get married and guess to who? To Angelik who lives on the new side road!'

Angelik was a spinster who lived outside the village in a stone house. She'd been a maid in town, and later worked for the notary here in the village. When he died, she received a legacy. With it she built her house and bought shares. She invited her sister to live with her, a widow with three children. The children are married and live here, there and everywhere. Her sister has had dropsy in her legs for years and has to drive in a special carriage.

'What do you think, Root?

'Well, father, what am I supposed to think?

'What? That you'll lead the life of a burgomaster, a house of your own, no longer having to work. Do you see him there, Root, Mr Verhaegen in his Sunday best every day! And a fat cigar in his mouth! I'll pop in for a gin or something! Just you wait, my man. You won't profit from the good life alone!'

'And what about my four children?' I asked (At that time there were four still at home, our blind Amelieken, our Mon, but he was going to marry when he got out of the army, so I don't count him, our Stan who was fifteen at the time, Liesken and Amedeken, my first child by Frisine; the second had died of measles a year after the death of Frisine).

'Those four children will stay with you,' said the priest. 'Don't worry about the children. Didn't Angelik look after her sister's three children with great charity and ensure them a good future? So it's nothing new for her to be confronted with a full household. And isn't it because she cared so well for the notary's children that he left her such a splendid legacy. Her sister will naturally go into the hospital, because her condition's getting worse and requires a nun to look after her. You don't look happy, Root?'

'Yes, yes... but she scarcely knows me... just by sight.'

'She knows you very well. She definitely likes you a lot. Of course, Root, we're not talking here about young love, man. This must be a marriage born of friendship. You're both getting on for sixty and then your wild youth is behind you. You need rest now, do what you want and enjoy. You've worked hard and long enough...'

But why does she want me and not someone without children?

'Why... Because you want her!'

'I? I? I scarcely know her. I've never thought about it!'

'I thought about it for you, Root. Don't you understand?I fixed things well. She's fallen in love with you because I told her you want her!'

'Ha! You're taking me for a fool,' I cried. 'You've been lying to this woman! Behind my back you've...'

'For the sake of the children! It's permitted to lie for other people's good, Root! Ha! Ha! Ha! Don't you find me a good marriage broker?'

'First prize, for turning someone's life upside down! Fine tricks, to fit me up with a woman whom I must carry across my threshold as my wife.'

'You won't carry anything into your own house. Or do think she'll come and live here in this cottage? Ha! Ha! Silly man! When I do something, I don't do it by halves, you'll go and live with her, you'll sell everything and you'll move into her house with your children!'

'The children too?'

'Of course! You see, man, I fixed things properly, hey.'

'But how can I work my field, if I no longer have a cowshed, no animals, no...!'

'Your field? You leave it where it is. That's for your Mon. He won't have to look any further for a house. You can start farming for your pleasure. The land that goes with Angelik's house is quite enough to keep you busy, thirty poles, I think...'

'I'll have dug that over in a day!'

'Then you give yourself a week or two weeks. Now you'll see others work! Lucky man! Playing the third wife and her posh husband! Every day hearty food, beer with your meals. Lying in, going for walks, planting flowers, reading your paper by the stove! Let it freeze as hard as it likes, you'll be out of the cold. Done with worries and fretting whether it will rain or not, done with fear of slugs, caterpillars and moles. Done with fear for the children, whether they eat on time and have clean smock on! You're going to be a gentleman, people will take their hats off to you. "Good day, Mr Root!"' The priest took his hat off to me, patted me on the shoulder, and began again. 'Now you must admit that I'm your best friend, hey, Root! People will envy you…'

He said all kinds of other things. I was flummoxed. What is it about me that women like me so much? I've always thought of myself as a scarecrow. That Angelik must be man-crazy to want me, a peasant farmer with four children! I can't get over it. Not a marriage of love but of friendship. But I would have to sleep with this skinny woman. And leave my house, a dilapidated cottage, it's true, but my life has been lived under this roof. My life formed a cloud between those walls. In another house I'd dry up and let myself go. Like a plant that's brought into the greenhouse out of the open air. And leave my animals. And my field! But seen from another point of view, I should be free at a stroke from that hound in the chateau. The old mademoiselle is in Heaven, at least if all those masses helped her to get in. Now Coco is the boss, that slob who's going to teach me to plant celery one day and who himself can't tell endives from spinach. A person would marry the devil to be rid of him. Leave my field, my field that I Have made so good and soft and lush, that knows me... that I can talk to. But to be able rest for a change, with drinking money in my pocket, a bottle of the best in the cupboard, and especially the children out of worry and deprivation... oh, that that woman has to be Angelik, as thin as a rake.

'Lucky dog, and you're still not laughing,' cried the priest.

'It's too much all at once, father. Why didn't you tell me about it a little at a time...'

'A spoonful every hour. You're not a child any more, Root!'

'And what am I supposed to do now?...'

'I don't give lessons in love. But she'll come here for milk, perhaps as soon as tomorrow. Then you'll talk about the weather, you'll give her a flower, they always like that, and one word will lead to another. You mustn't start at once, the business will come closer every day...'

'And what must I say?'

'Good grief, Root! How can you be so dried up. What did you say to our Fien and Frisine?'

'Not much, father, where the conversation led, but it came from the heart...'

'Then this will come from the heart too. First get to know one another a bit. You see, Root, life is no laughing matter, but it's smiling on you.

'Don't be wet about it. Don't gamble with your happiness. I've now informed you and you must be a man!'

I watched him go: it was as if I were dreaming... A third wife. Angelik.

And he didn't even ask me if I agreed! Yes, a wife was necessary. It wasn't like a funfair at our place. Our Irma came to do the scrubbing on Saturdays. She came back home, and the others did too. I had thought, after they had misjudged Frisine so, that I would wring the neck of the first one that crossed my threshold, but when you hear them say father again, the rage subsides. A wife was needed. No one offered to come into our nest, I myself didn't dare think about it. I did not want to take on a maid, because I know myself too well. I careered on working hard and staying poor. Those past five years were hard years, like a clumsy dream. I know only one thing: I took pleasure in my field. And suddenly Angelik is standing in my path. And now suddenly there's an end to farming and I must leave my field!

That affects me so deeply, that I can't do a stroke of work that day and keep letting my eyes wander over my field.

How beautifully it lies there, well kneaded, pure and grateful. Every grain of sand has passed through my hand, each handful of earth has felt my pulse. It listens to me, I have made it humble and mild, and it gives me what I desire of it. But I listen to it too, its cares are my cares, its pleasure is my pleasure! I fed it with cess and manure, always the best, I always gave it the best seed and the most select plants; I looked after it and cleared it of weeds and pests. I've often given it a few ladles more cess, about which a farmer is so niggardly and rightly so, purely from affection and generosity, because I know that it likes it so much. It was a constant silent conversation between me and the field and on Sundays there was time and I spoke aloud to it: 'Come on, men, and let's have your turnips, hey! Show me you have better manners than the Oxhead's!'

Yes, yes I enjoyed my field and still do although it brought me poverty. And now I shall have to leave that field for the sake of the children, and also for my own sake, because I'm fed up with poverty. A good life is not a bad thing and after all I can't go on farming all my life. It has to come to an end. Our Mon will be pleased when he comes on leave on Sunday. I got the field for him on a platter, it will pass from father to son, as in the Old Testament; it will remain in the family. So I can relax about that. Angelik... I close my eyes when I think of Angelik, so as not to see her. I want to marry blindly, just as I believe blindly. But let me curse for a moment, that lightens the heart. She has a good character, she looks good-hearted, a shame she's so skinny. But if our Fien or Frisine had been skinny, I would still have taken them. Skinny or not, marriage! Worse accidents have happened. Don't play with your happiness!

She came for milk.

Our blind Amelieken gives her milk. I sat in the cowshed watching, from between the legs of our cow. My heart was trembling like a reed with shyness.

And shame. Fool, I said to myself, be brave and come out of your shell!

'And you can't see at all, Amelieken, poor thing...' I hear her say, 'that must be sad.'

'It's as good as if I can see,' said the child laughing. 'I know everything here, from the smell, from the air, from hearing. When I cough I can hear from the echo if there someone more or less there or if there is something in the way... of course I'm used to it here...'

'Poor thing,' said Angelik, and she stroked our Amelieken's hair and cheeks... 'I shall pray for you a lot...'

You see, that moves the father of a blind child. I got up and when I heard her say: 'Isn't your father at home?' I came out of the cowshed...

She lowered her eyes like a woman in love. Of course, the priest had said I was crazy about her. But what was I supposed to say now?

'Can you come and dig over the soil in my garden?'

'Yes, yes, Angelik...'

She laughed and shook her small, thin head.

'Can you come tomorrow?...'

Tomorrow I had to sow. Don't gamble with your happiness, I hear the priest say in my heart and I said, 'Yes, I'll be there.'

She said a little more about the plight of our Amelieken, while she wanted to read the friendliness in my face, which was not in or on it, and that seemed to make her sad.

'Till tomorrow then,' she said suddenly, like someone who was about to cry and she had gone without looking round.

I watched her go. That was the woman I was about to abuse to make myself and my children happy. So much play-acting in the world!

Oh yes, the priest said: 'And you give her a flower.'

I quickly had Amelieken run after her with a peony.

'From our Dad,' said the child.

That seemed really to please her, because she waved with the flower, smelt it and waved again.

'She seems to be a good person,' said our Amelieken.

That sentence of our Amelieken's filled me with confidence. With this sentence my doubt was over and my marriage decided.

The next day I went there to work.

'Come and have a glass of beer first.'

I took my clogs off. It was like a house in town, squeaky clean, with of white and black tiles, a Mechelen stove with lots of nickel that gleamed like a mirror, holy figures on the mantelpiece, and the walls made of stones like in the parlours in town. Her sister sat behind the stove, a fat woman with a lop-sided mouth.

'Have a look at the rooms,' said Angelik. Two rooms one after another with wooden floors. 'They're going to have linoleum on top,' she said. On the tables were squares of crochet work and the chairs were covered in red velvet. There was a portrait album on the table, she opened it, there were no portraits inside, but, good heavens, a delicate music box began to play. The second room had beautiful wallpaper, one parrot after another, all luxurious.

'Oh, Amelieken, my puss,' I thought, 'when she sits on those velvet chairs! One can do a lot with money!'

'Upstairs there are two more big rooms,' said Angelik, and two nice attic rooms in case we have visitors, and she looked at me with embarrassment and understanding.

Look,' she said, pointing to a glass vase with a ribbon round it. In it was the peony.

I tried to be friendly and to speak. 'I've got plenty more of those,' I said.

She poured beer from a bottle. 'My sister is going to the hospital,' she said with a sigh that required an answer and she added, 'then I'll be all alone here...'

'Alone is just alone,' I said and she laughed at my eyes, as if to say, I shan't be alone for long.

I set to work in the garden. A garden with a partial wall and for the rest a hedge and a gate at the bottom. I didn't like it. It seemed to me like a prison. This would be my field from now on! I, who was used to seeing things hours away in the distance and could flourish happy and proud beside my field, past potatoes, grain, vegetables, through the meadow, over canals, past

154

bushes, around my house, in the cowshed. Now my field was reduced to a few little plots, the view and the path cut off by hedge and wall, with the only livestock six plucked chickens without a cock!

She came and stood by me. I said nothing and went on digging. After having sighed a few times, she said: 'You're right, alone is just alone...' and afterwards: 'I've often had a chance to marry, but didn't want to. Now I regret it. I like a big household.'

Suddenly she said: 'The priest is a good friend of yours, your best...'

'Yes,' I said drily. 'I tell him everything.'

But she snapped at that word the way a pike snaps at a little fish.

'He told me everything,' she said and looked at me penetratingly. I came out in a sweat. Now the cat was out of the bag, and so quickly?

I bent my head. I couldn't say: 'He lied to you!' So, I said nothing and bowed my head. But she must have taken this stupid gesture as an admission, because she laid her skinny hand on mine and said with a lump in her throat: 'I love you greatly too, Root, as much you do me...'

I know,' I said, still looking down.

'Did the priest talk much about me?'

'No... no... just a bit... after I, after I...'

I couldn't get the word out, but she spoke it for me:

'Of course, he can't keep quiet. It was quite a blow, wasn't it? After you said that you would so like me to be your wife, he was often here. To tell the truth,

Root, I had never thought of you, but since the priest spoke about you in such glowing terms my thoughts focused on you. I thought about it for a long time. But you see, I must attach myself to someone. I can't and don't want to stay alone, and I love children, and it will do me good to hear children living and moving around me again. I will love them so much, Root!'

That broke the ice. I got up.

'That's good of you, Angelik.'

She wiped her tears away. 'You can tell the priest,' she sighed, 'that I accept your proposal…'

Yes, that was what she said to me.

But before she drained the potatoes that noon, she herself had gone and said to him herself like a flash that she had given her consent to my proposal. And you mustn't swear about that!

The priest was glad. The children were glad. The neighbours congratulated me. Only our Amelieken was gloomy. She had nothing against Angelik. If Angelik came and lived in my cottage, she was all in favour. But now she had to leave the house where she knew everything as well as if she could see. I often said: 'She has eyes in her fingertips.' She was familiar with everything in the house. She knew her passage, the cowshed, she milked like a Bertha, my daughter-in-law, she knew every animal, she where everything was, she knew her way to the field, but once outside, she stood there like a lost lamb.

'Dad,' she said, 'I'm going to be lost at Angelik's place, like someone who goes blind.'

I didn't say: me too, child, but: 'We'll get used to it, child. I shall have plenty of time there, and I'll teach you everything, and you will go walking a lot with me, just the two of us…'

Our Mon was naturally glad, he was soon due to leave the army and would then marry Franelle's daughter. So everything could stay as it was. At the chateau they also approved of the arrangement. Changing personnel was a small matter for them, provided the money remained the same.

The banns were read at the end of May. Angelik had not yet profited much from my great love, which the priest had described so glowingly. I couldn't get over what I was about to do. I constantly stood leaning on my spade thinking. I could no longer work peacefully, I stood looking at my animals, I wandered into the barn, pulled the loft ladder up, went and sat in the cart shed, peered and dreamt of my field. I devoured it with my eyes. And I was supposed to leave all this. Your body and soul are shaped, kneaded by it; your blood has come to flow in time with it; it is your breath… Damn!

Angelik had the tailor come round for a new black suit. She also sent for a stiff shirt and a stiff collar. I had never worn a collar before. The two times that I got married I wore a silk scarf… and now I would have to wear a collar every day. 'I shall make a gentleman of you,' she had said. Ha, if it weren't for the children I wouldn't get married. I sometimes had to go and stand in my field, alone to be able to swear properly... at myself.

I brooded, constantly weighing the pros and cons. I occasionally spoke my mind to the priest. 'Bah,' he said. 'before you've been married a week you'll laugh at your former life. Everything is habit...'

That gave me fresh heart. And I thought of the fine life.

The children were allowed to come and eat at Angelik's, and they really tucked in! Every day meat and eggs, dammit! It truly came from a good and generous heart. I had to admire the woman.

Whatever was usable of mine and the children's was taken to Angelik's house, the rest she would buy in. And so the wedding day approached inevitably. It oppressed my heart like a great storm.

Tomorrow I ventured into the sea of love for the third time.

God save me!

I couldn't swallow a bite. I went to confess towards dusk, the priest congratulated me. 'It lies heavy on my heart I said.

'Tomorrow it will be over,' he said.

I didn't go home. I couldn't stand to be anywhere I was so harassed. I had to have air, lots of distance before me and around me, to be able to go and keep going. A farmer always winds up on his field.

I remember it well, there was a sharp crescent moon in the sky. Tomorrow it will be good weather for sowing carrots, I thought. Nonsense! Your days of sowing carrots are over! I took a handful of earth in my hand and examined it.

'The things a man has to go through before he dies,' I said. 'We search for happiness and here it lies at my feet.'

Wasn't I happy with my field? You bet I was. The adversity that I had, did not come from the field, it came from people and myself. That's life. Yes, the field has always been my salvation in adversity, and has strengthened my heart. Without a field, from tomorrow living with Angelik. I could still encounter adversity, and I'll have no more field to console me.

To have to leave such a beautiful field, drenched with my sweat and my thoughts. We have become one. Each fruit is something of mine. Each fruit seemed to me to grow better through my thoughts than through manure. I let my eyes wander over my crops from here to over there and back and forth. Oh, if it rains now I shan't be able to be glad or fearful. My eye and my spirit will no longer be able to delight as the plough carves the beautiful earth into gleaming scales. Why don't they cut my arms off!

I got home late. I still had the earth in my hand.

I was getting frightened, called Amelieken from upstairs.

'Go to sleep, child.'

'I can't sleep, Dad,' and there was a sob in her voice.

'Neither can I,' called Liesken, 'I keep thinking about the party.

'I went into the cowshed again with my lantern. I intended to wander round the whole place... But that would only make it worse. Anyway, I was allowed to go on farming for another week, as our Mon finally leaves the army next Sunday. He was coming tomorrow for the party. It was my duty to go to see Angelik again, and I did so. A nun from the hospital and friend were busy cooking and plucking chickens. Angelik showed me her dress, dark blue with black lace. Right, till tomorrow then.' We shook hands. I have to do it anyway, so why pull ugly faces? And I pulled a very friendly one, the friendliest, and she got tears in her eyes again. A good woman!

No question of sleeping. I pulled my trousers on again and sat at the door for a smoke. It was close, I fell asleep. I was woken by my pipe which fell and broke. The day appeared in the sky. I smelled my house, I sniffed its scent. One never smells one's own house, except when one's been away from it for a long time, after eight months' imprisonment, for example. And through the smelling of that smell, a tear came into my eye, a curse into my mouth (and I had shortly to go to communion), a rage and sorrow into my heart, and I began to shout: No! no! never! I won't do it… not even for a million… Damn!… Damn you with your good heart… keep it… Keep it. Leave me alone… I won't do it! I sobbed, stamped, like an angry child…

Our Amelieken came. 'What is it, Dad?…'

And I told her. 'I want to do it for your happiness, but I can't, I can't.'

'But Daddy, daddy, what will people say…and the priest?…' she cried helplessly.

'I don't give two hoots about any of them. Do you want to go and live with Angelik?…'

'No, Dad, but I'm doing it for you and the children.'

'And I for you and the children. I needn't do it for you, because you'd rather not go… And Our Dear Lord will look after the others.' I suddenly became calm. 'Quick,' I said, 'go to the priest, get him out of bed, and tell him. That I'm not marrying for any reason!'

'But Daddy,' she argued.

'Go!' And she went. She knew her way of course, and before ten minutes have passed, the priest will be here giving me a sermon. Let him come! I shall tell him everything. I was ready. My blood was boiling. I see them both hurrying along over there. I must have gone as white as a sheet. My courage sank into my shoes. I felt lost. He's going to win with his words… God be with me… Like a thief I ran away and hid in the wardrobe.

I heard him say angrily: 'What manners! And the meal. The whole party And the family who are coming! What a disgrace!

'What a disgrace! What that chap does to me… He must, he must, do you understand, Amelieken? He must… Poor Angelik!'

I don't understand how they did not hear my heartbeat through the wardrobe. Pounding like a mallet.

I heard our Amelieken calling outside and in:

'Dad, Dad!...' They went outside, and back inside, and he gave free rein to his anger.

When they were outside again, I crept out of the wardrobe and went out by the back way. Suddenly I hear shouting.

'Root! Root! It's me, the priest!... Root! Do it for the children! Stop, I tell you, stop! Don't you understand what a disgrace, what a...'

If I look round I am just a bird to Angelik, I thought. And I walked on, always, till I no longer heard his words, and I was still walking, always walking without looking round, into the woods and laughed, laughed, saved and freed. Always walking, walking, walking...

I had my field back! My field! My field!

X

AND now I sit here alone with our Amelieken. The rest are married with lots of kids. Such is life. Each has his turn. I give them my blessing. But I'm not dead yet!

Christ on the Cross stands waiting against the wall to be planted on my grave. I'll plant him on my grave, or better have him planted, because I need him most.

He's not completely finished yet. I have a premonition that if I finish him, I'll be finished too. And I want to stay alive! The older I get the greedier I get to live. Not from fear of death, but from attachment to life. I think life is beautiful and good. Still, I don't live in luxury. Of course, my area of land, since I have been working alone, has become more than five times smaller, but I must still toil and slave hard to have a supply of bread. We have only one cow left, one pig and a dozen chickens. That's all my livestock. The cow must give milk, pull the plough, and take the manure to the village at night. At the same time it's my horse.

Still, life is beautiful, at least for a peasant farmer. It's so secure and fixed: the nights follow the days, the moon is always on time, the change of seasons, which come back every time, like before, and yet are always new and different, takes place with a firm hand. For a town gentleman between four cushioning walls that's of no account, but for a farmer it's life. Those motions treat and work the fields, they keep the heart and soul taut.

The farmer's life attaches me like a root, after my name, to life. It's as if I will and can never die.

When I sow I never think: Will I still be here to mow! I will mow! The sowing and the mowing and the sowing again are like a circle that death cannot penetrate. He has no right to me, as long as I'm working.

The Oxhead, he's still alive, the rogue, the Twister and Franelle hang over a bench for days on end, outside in the wind, droning on and complaining about the bad times, about gout and their lame feet, so that the spittle runs over their chin.

Are they farmers?

They laugh at me for continuing to work.

'Come and sit with and have a rest,' they ask me, 'you still won't make a fortune with that.'

As if I work to get rich! I could have become a fighter in a strong man booth. I was strong enough for it. I followed the call of my farmer's blood, I work because I can't help it, because I have to from deep in my heart, and because I like it.

I could sit on a bench all day just as well as them! Our Irma would like nothing better than to have me come and live with her. There I would have all the food I could eat. But I want to be free and farm, and to farm the way I like, in the old true splendid way.

Such men, I don't understand it, don't know the pleasure of the peasant farmer's life. That pleasure isn't to laugh and sit at your ease with a cigar in your chops.

Watching your leeks grow. The pleasure lies in the waiting. In carefully waiting to see how the seed germinates, how the crop will fare, and while you mow one thing, the other is already sown, and so on endlessly. I can't understand how there are farmers who after they have sown can leave their land voluntarily, and let others do the harvesting. A real farmer couldn't do that. The seed lies as if on his own heart, he can't leave it…That's why I think I didn't marry Angelik back then. A shame for her. The woman did not survive the shame for long. People say she died of it. I had blotted my copybook badly with everyone. My children were angry, but that was because of Angelik's lovely money, the neighbour thought I was a Judas, the people at the chateau, where Angelik occasionally went to cook, grumbled and threatened to cancel my tenancy, and even with my best friend, the priest, who had brokered the deal, I had put my foot in it. He no longer came to see us and I avoided him. I no longer dared to go to confession with him. He saw me in church when he preached, but he pretended not to see me. It was the assistant pastor who came for the St Peter's penny. You couldn't say the priest is angry. No, it was just that we no longer saw each other alone.

So years passed. I was very sorry, I had lost a good friend in him, who could console me and cheer me up when I needed it. And I was often ready to go and speak to him, but of course I never managed to. He became ill and let his hair grow. He always sat in his garden reading a book or listening to the birds.

In the winter he sent for me. He was in bed. There had been half a metre of snow, and it was still snowing, I went with an anxious heart, because a sermon awaited me.

'Have a seat, Root!'

I had to sit by his bed.

He put his hand on my shoulder.

'Do you see it snowing, Root!' he asked. 'That's how the souls fall out of Heaven, from God's hand. I've never yet read how many people have lived since the creation, and certainly how many will live in future.

'It will be a lot, Root.

'Look at the flakes falling, that's how all the souls come down to earth... Is it now not all the same whether you are this or that flake? And yet every flake is different. Have you ever seen snow through a magnifying glass, Root?

I have, it's all stars, triangles and mathematical figures. No two from all those billions are identical. All snowflakes will melt again into water, become mist and be sucked up again high in the sky, where they came from. That gives me food for thought.

So every soul is like a snowflake, each one shaped differently. We descend cover the earth for a while and generally speaking return. What do I care whether I'm a flake that fell on the earth a thousand years ago or falls now or within a thousand years from now. The case remains the same. We melt anyway. If I'd fallen a thousand years ago, then I would already have had my existence, and would already have been relieved of my load. I have a great homesickness for Heaven, Root, that's why I became a priest, and that's why I ask Our Dear Lord to let me melt soon… Do you understand that, Root?'

'Yes,' I said, 'that's a beautiful meditation.'

'So all nature is a mirror for the soul, Root,' and he told me lots more beautiful things about death, hell and Heaven, of which I only understood half and only half listened to, as I was waiting for the launch of the rocket about Angelik.

'Did you have a good crop of potatoes, Root?,' he asked suddenly, 'and is the milk still so good. The goodness of milk depends not on the animal, that is just a funnel, a sieve; good milk depends on good grass. That little meadow, from which you always gave the first cut to your animals, imparted that taste and that splendour to the milk…'

Now it comes, I thought.

'I still have that meadow, father…'

'The farmer's trade is a fine one, isn't it, Root… I've always enjoyed being among farmers. In the spring when I'm right again and mobile, you'll see me again in your cowshed, man! And how is Amelieken?'

And while I told him with my eyes mostly fixed on the carpet (for I didn't dare look at the priest too closely, thinking each time that he would start talking about Angelik), he had fallen asleep. Or so it seemed. At first I stood there dawdling and then left on tiptoe. I said to the maid downstairs: 'He's asleep. He fell asleep while I was talking.'

'Oh, that will do him good,' she said, 'he hasn't slept a wink in two weeks. I'll go and have a look shortly.' She pours me a gin, and says as I leave: 'You must come back, he so likes talking to you.'

I went homeward through the snow. You could scarcely see your arm in front of you, so thickly was the snow falling. These were no longer flakes but lumps. Suddenly I hear anxious shouting : 'Root! Root!' It was the voice of the maid.

'Yes!' I shouted 'What is it?'

'Quick! Quick! Come and see, the pastor is dead, I think… the pastor…'

While I was telling him my story he had died. The maid had gone to look full of happiness, but she noticed something odd about his colour, full of alarm she spoke to him. He was dead.

To tell the truth, it may be ridiculous, but I cried like one does less than four times in one's life.

In him I have lost a good friend, the best and he still wanders often through my thoughts, and then we talk to each other. So everything goes, so everything melts, one before, the other after.

Now I have only our Amelieken. The others, who are married, I don't count. A married child is only half a child. Amelieken is a garden of jollity and goodness. She's blind and perhaps that's why she's so good and cheerful. She actually lives in another world: something that we sighted people do not know and cannot understand. I don't pity her. She always says: How unfortunate it must be not to be able to hear! Rather not see than not be able to smell the flowers and not to be able to hear the birds singing.

She keeps things light and melodious around me. She consoles me and makes my heart glitter with gladness, like the sun in a windowpane. Not through fine words or sayings, but through her attitude, through something that through the sound of her voice comes from her heart, and fills your heart with peace, even if you sit shaking and trembling on your chair with toothache. Happiness comes off her like a good smell, so that you sometimes start to wish, though I don't do it, that you could be blind too.

Our Amelieken is really a blessing to me in my old age, a wonderful gift, for which I thank Our Dear Lord especially!

But I thank You for so much, O Lord! For everything! My heart and my mouth never cease praising you!

Lord God, You sent me into the world to sow and mow. And I did so and it made me happy.

On the other hand You did not spare me, and from time to time gave me a few slaps in the face. A good father doesn't spare the rod.

It might have been better if we'd spoken about it together; as it was, I often didn't know why I took a hard knock, and then I grumbled and thundered at you.

It's been bad, very bad, but it's over. And what's over, I won't have to deal with anymore. Let it thunder on someone else now, I've had my share. My hair has turned white in places because of it and the rosary of my back has bent forward.

But I'm still alive! And if I occasionally close my eyes to reflect on my life, I don't think of the dark and sad things that have jolted and trodden on me, the scars have healed, the pain has been forgotten, and I see only the beautiful things. How the seasons rustle past with bright days full of colour and sun, our Fien and Frisine come out from behind a cloud, both with wings on, and laugh at me while I am sowing. Old age is like a sieve, it lets only the sun through, and it gilds memory. Dammit, that's just as well, what else should a man do, if he felt himself rejected and deceived by God for days on end! The good memories lead one to experience those pleasant hours once more, and get down to work again.

O Lord let me go on working for a long time. Let it last for a long time! It's so good and beautiful and I'm not yet homesick enough for Your Heaven to lay down my spade.

O my God, I thank You for this open field, over which you stand invisibly in the highest heaven. I thank you at night when I hear you rustling among the stars. I thank you for the spring, the summer, the autumn and the winter, since they are four gestures of Your goodness, and the enjoyment and fruit are always the same and yet always as fresh as for the first time.

I thank You for the rainbows that You stretch across the thunderclouds, for the rain that refreshes my crops, for the sun that sucks them out of the ground, for the winds that blow the evil away, and make the windmills turn, and for the snow that tucks in the winter corn. Thanks to the moon when it rises or sets, it always does something good if one knows its catlike tricks.

Thanks to the falling leaves, they are manure, thanks to the grass, which becomes milk! Thanks to the clouds, the brook, the pollard willows, and all the crops, both the beets and the radishes; Your breath gives them the will to live, their proper taste, colour and size. Thanks to Your labours day and night. You are our help, Your kingdom slaves away like a farmhand.

I thank You, Lord, in Heaven, on earth and everywhere.

Thanks to you in the Holy Sacrament, whose host is related to the same corn we eat in our sandwiches and that we worshippers surround in the procession through the fields with candlelight and incense. Thanks even to the Jesus that I carved from wood, and that explored the great darkness and light of my heart.

I thank You, Lord… On harps and strings! It says in my prayer book, but I have nothing but a bugle, on which I can only play a waltz and a death march. I thank You with all my passionate heart! Out of all the fullness of my soul.

And let Your Root in return work many more years on Your field (which unfortunately also belongs to the chateau) by the sweat of my brow!

Thanks in advance!

TRANSLATOR'S NOTE

FELIX TIMMERMANS (1886-1947) was born in Lier in a rural area of Flanders known as the Kempen. His early work, for example *Schemeringen van de dood* (Intimations of Death, 1910) was pessimistic and concerned, not to say obsessed, with the occult, but he won international acclaim with *Pallieter* (1916), a life-affirming, carefree Burgundian tale of peasant life.

Boerenpsalm (A Peasant Farmer's Psalm, 1935), first serialised in the literary magazine *De Nieuwe Gids* (The New Guide), was Timmermans' first book to employ first-person narrative, thus adding to its directness. It is also characterised by extensive use of the writer's own native Kempen dialect. The work's vitalism assumes almost mythical proportions in its depiction of farming life. The novel was three times adapted for the stage and in 1989 was filmed by Roland Verhavert.

PV

Milton Keynes UK
Ingram Content Group UK Ltd.
UKHW040843230923
429253UK00004B/84